THE BLOOD OF THE SIBILLINI

A novel by
Francesco Eleuteri

Translated by Phoebe Leed and Nathan Neel

Rondini Press

PROLOGUE

Apennine District — Umbria-Marche
Sibillini Mountains National Park
Province of Ascoli Piceno
Township of Montegallo
One of the Twenty-one Villages
Autumn 19XX
7:38 PM

The television was talking about his little sister. A week had passed since they'd taken her away. For her own good, they said. But what he heard on television didn't seem "good." Giuseppe wasn't an "A" student. In fact he was a bit of a dim bulb, but he understood what the talking heads on the TV were saying.

"... the investigation is continuing regarding the serious case of sexual abuse within the community preschool of Montegallo, a small mountain center in the province of Ascoli Piceno. The victim, a five year old girl, is the daughter of a farming couple who pressed charges against the teacher. The accusation was based on various drawings done by the little girl, as interpreted by a psychologist at the hospital of Ascoli Piceno. According to the family's attorney, the little girl remains in a psychological state that raises serious concerns. Her condition is presumably due to the trauma she has experienced. The victim has retreated into silence ..."

Giuseppe was alone at home. His parents had gone to visit his little sister at the institute where she was recuperating on the advice of the lawyer Bonanni. The lawyer had offered to represent the family of the victim for free. Giuseppe didn't understand why his sister would be better off at the institute, but his mother had told him that the lawyer said it was necessary for her wellbeing... and to get more money.

Huh! Giuseppe didn't understand. He was angry, staring at the photo that was being shown on TV of a face with the eyes covered by a black band.

"The teacher, Michela Angeletti, is under house arrest while awaiting clarification of the evidence, which she contests. She denies any involvement in the case."

Giuseppe knew that face well. It wasn't enough to cover her eyes to conceal her identity from him. He was fifteen years old. He didn't go to school anymore — he had never liked it — but he wasn't stupid. The teacher had done something bad to his little sister.

He lowered his gaze to the plate that his mother had prepared for him. The face of the teacher gave way to a slice of meat that was already cold.

With his left hand, he took up the fork.

With his right hand, the knife.

FIRST PART

A jolt. A sudden loss of breath. He sat upright with a jerk, a "no" strangled in his throat, in the midst of an unmade bed.

A terrible way to wake up in the middle of the night. Maurizio turned on the bedside light and grabbed a bottle of water. He gulped down half of it, cleansing his mouth of the dry taste of the nightmare.

He got up and opened the drawer of his writing desk, taking in one hand the documents that certified the purchase, while with the other he wiped his face, beaded with sweat. For some seconds he leafed through the pages one-handed; the other was soaked and he didn't want to ruin the papers.

The mirror on the opposite wall reflected a tall gaunt figure. His eyes, red from interrupted sleep, never left the all-important papers, while he tugged on the light growth of beard that framed his face with the fingers unencumbered by the precious pages.

It all seemed to be in order. The house had been bought from the one and only owner, the real estate carried no mortgage, the price had been paid in full, and the deed had been routinely registered by the notary. So what the hell was this "Ecosystem" that was claiming the property, stating it had acquired it from the true owner?

In the meantime Maurizio had renovated it, making it as close as possible to the dream of his boyhood. Back then he had gone on vacation in these mountains with his parents; every year they rented a different place, and he had always looked at this particular near-ruin with the certainty that one day it would be beautiful, and above all, it would be his.

Thirty years later he had succeeded. But suddenly a lawyer who claimed to represent the company Ecosystem had proposed an agreement in which his client would basically repurchase the house at the price paid, plus an extra amount for his trouble. Should this agreement not be accepted, the lawyer was in a position — or so he said — to demonstrate the invalidity of Maurizio's purchase, given that the house had not been bought from the legitimate owner — which, on the contrary, Ecosystem had taken the care to do.

Given the necessity of moving ahead quickly, Ecosystem was prepared to lose a little money.

Maurizio had no intention of accepting.

He replaced his dream in the drawer, being careful not to crumple it, and went back to bed hoping for a respite from troubled thoughts.

Rome
Theater of the Satyrs
Friday, June 15, 20XX
9:34 PM

The lights in the hall went down. Darkness. The music came up. Applause.

On stage, in the spotlight, Tony Liberati, actor and author of the performance now underway. The music hushed. The actor paused. A long pause. Too long. Silence. Then the single phrase, "I'm not doing it."

He bowed in front of the pit, waved, and left.

He was finished. Enough. Over.

Whistles, insults. A couple of spectators tried to pursue him backstage. The theater ushers intervened followed by the director who, with a heavy heart, announced that the ticket price would be refunded. Every evening, for three weeks, the actor had brought to the stage of the Theater of the Satyrs of Rome his latest work, "The Pleasures of Old Walter," a sort of social satire in which the habits and caprices of the Italian upper class were held up to ridicule.

But he was indifferent to the success he had achieved. He was physically and mentally exhausted.

Because of this he had chosen to stop the performances three evenings earlier than the Sunday which had been advertised on the billboards. He made the decision suddenly, a few seconds before going on stage. While looking in the mirror and adjusting the microphone, he realized he couldn't do it anymore. He decided this against the interests of the theater that was hosting him and the producers who had invested in the show. He decided on his own, as always, even if the decision put him in default with respect to the other parties involved. Their stake appeared obvious and sacrosanct, that is, the critical success and the box office receipts—which were, moreover, greater than expected. On the contrary, Tony's motivation found no justification and seemed to be a whim. The play was the actor's creation, but the other side threatened legal action.

Friday, the last show.

Applauding him, in the second row, was his eternal friend Maurizio Verdimani. He had followed Tony since the difficult beginnings in the tiny theaters staged in Roman basements, where the so-called "off-off" self gratifyingly curled itself around its intellectualism, dreaming of the avante garde of Europe and overseas, but remaining bogged down in the lack of attention and money that the governing Italian culture always reserved for them. Not that Tony Liberati could have become a star, but he had found his niche, his portion of true esteem on the part of the working theater crowd. He was able to support himself in a more than dignified manner with his art—or with his "artisanship," as he often liked to say—thus he felt gratified.

Lately it wasn't enough. But that wasn't the point.

Maurizio waited for him at the exit. They had made plans to go out to eat, not having seen each other for months.

Maurizio often worked late, lost in the tapes, the films, the digital versions of RAI's television archives on the Via Salaria, where he was employed. Beyond that, he didn't like the nightclubs, the parties, social life in general. In contrast to Tony who, partly for pleasure, partly to observe the human species, was a devotee not only of the fashionable clubs but of nightlife in general. From the streets to the suburban bars to the intellectual salons which, even though ridiculous in his eyes, nonetheless constituted lavish lairs of young women easy to fascinate.

The chance to get together and have a friendly chat was grabbed in midflight, in the literal meaning of the word. Tony escaped through the side door, covered in a black cloak unearthed from a costume trunk and wearing a platinum wig.

Maurizio waited for him in his car with the motor running and all his senses on high alert. A group of ferocious ex-fans were waiting outside the theater. At half past midnight the two friends were seated in a little restaurant in Piazza Mattei, facing the fountain of the turtle; with a not very summery plate of spaghetti "cacio e pepe" and an extremely icy bottle of Greco di Tufo.

"I've passed the last hour waiting for you and thinking about where we would eat a good "cacio e pepe.""

Tony merely gave him an eloquent glance so Maurizio backpedaled, "Come on, I was only joking! Anyway, at least I remembered this place...I really did crave some of this spaghetti."

"Yeah, all right, but did you like the show? What do you say? I think it went well, every night I got positive reviews, and the fact that it ran three weeks with a full house every night means that the word of mouth was good, but..."

"Tony, you didn't put on the show. Or actually you did a different one. Pitiful!"

"Ah yes, you didn't see it. So I'll tell you about it."

"Eat! 'Cacio e pepe' is disgusting if it gets cold. And then, excuse me, but don't you ever get tired of talking about work? That's why I never come to those horrible dinners full of actors, cabaret singers, directors, authors, and producers..."

"Enough already, I get it. Aside from the fact that I can't stand the theater crowd either, now it's you that's letting the spaghetti get cold. Eat! However, you're right. I'm tired. I'm stressed out. Get this, today I had an argument with a patrol of Carabinieri that had stopped me for a license check. On the seat next to me were the two guns I use in the show, blank pistols that I'd removed the red plug from so that they would look more realistic. And in fact, the gunshot did sound just like a real automatic."

"Result: they wanted to take me in. An endless discussion. As soon as they saw them they shoved two machine guns in my face, made me get out, and while they searched the car they kept me covered. I just about shit my pants. It was the straw that broke the camel's back."

"I got to the theater with no desire whatsoever to go on stage. For pity's sake, I like what I do, it's just that . . . who cares? Screw the theater . . . it's only good for those who do it."

"Now don't exaggerate,' Maurizio broke in. "What this means is that you really need some relaxation. Listen, do you remember Montegallo?"

"And how could I not remember it? For years you've hammered me with Montegallo—Mt. Rooster, or as the locals would say, Mt. Cock. Listen, I've learned the rap by heart: pearl of the Umbrian/Marche Apennines, on the slopes of Mt. Vettore facing the highest peak of the Sibillini Mountain chain, Montegallo consists of twenty-one villages, located as high as 1000 meters in altitude and almost all contained within the National Park of the Sibillini. The main village is Balzo. That's it, oh, and it's in the province of Ascoli Piceno."

"Damn, what a memory! The local tourist board should hire you. Anyway, what I want to tell you is that I finally bought a house in Montegallo, in the village of Astorara. It was basically a ruin in the middle of a green pasture with an oak tree next to it. The walls are stone, but the roof was gone. I bought it for a song and I've renovated it. It's driving me crazy. I want to enjoy myself a little and so I've decided to take two week vacation. Now. But I don't want to go there by myself, or with just anybody . . . so you have to come with me."

"But it's nowhere, a place in the middle of the mountains, there's nothing, no women, no bars, full of bugs and wild boars . . . and the chickens run around raw."

"Exactly. And by the way, they were quails."

"What do quails have to do with anything?"

"Yeah quails! They were quails. You just quoted Oscar Wilde who defined the countryside as 'a place where the quails run around raw.' You said chickens. You were mistaken."

"In any case, it's like that. I don't see myself hiking the trails with the desire of reaching the summit and then looking down. I prefer to stay down and see what's close by."

"Enough with the jokes. You said you needed rest. Here's your chance. Plus, we won't really be shut off from the world. If you get bored you can go down to Ascoli Piceno, half an hour by car."

"All right, I'll come. But on one condition."

"Which is?"

"Each of us takes his own car."

"If that makes you happy, fine. We'll leave tomorrow at noon. Let's meet in front of my house and then take the Via Salaria. In two hours we'll be there."

"There's one comforting thing."

"What's that?"

"I remember, from the two or three times you took me there, that I ate and drank very well, and almost never water."

"All right then, yes. Even in Montegallo they've discovered fire and sometimes they use it to make the meat better, eating it cooked, not just raw. Naturally, after they've carried it through the village and danced around the totem pole. Screw off..."

Tony gave a smile and dug into the 'cacio e pepe.' Maurizio, after staring at him for a few seconds added, "Can you please take off that horrible wig? It's making me lose my appetite."

Rome
The Piazza at the Pantheon
Outdoor Table at a Bar
Friday, June 15, 20XX

The waiter served an amaro, two coffees, and two glasses of mineral water. Silvio Forlan tasted the water as if he was sipping a vintage Barolo wine, then wrinkled his nose and called the waiter over.

"I would like to examine the bottle you poured this water from."

The waiter was perplexed, not sure he'd understood. "Is there something wrong, sir?"

"Don't worry about that. I only want to see the bottle."

Obviously irritated but trying not to show it, the boy left with the requisite smile and a "Right away, sir."

"You always make me look bad," Simona Coda commented with annoyance. Forlan's companion of more than ten years, she was a woman whose beauty stopped at an undefined age, with a spontaneous elegance by now self-conscious, with sophisticated tastes that bordered on whims, and with an unbounded passion for reading tarot cards. "Your obsession with water has become unbearable. But on the other hand the cards don't lie. Every time I consult them regarding your aura, they show a negative element that concerns your essence."

"What are you saying? What are you blathering about? You're paranoid with these cards. Water isn't my obsession, it's my work."

"In fact you're always thinking about work. Like tonight, we could've gone to the cinema or the theater and instead we have to go to dinner with that hick, Senator Cecchini."

"Shut up! He's been in the bathroom for ten minutes; he could come back any second. For me, he's valuable. He's going to do everything possible so that in his region, Le Marche..."

"Oh, so he's even a good ol' boy from Le Marche!"

"What do you know about people from Le Marche? However, if someone is interested in changing laws that have lasted for centuries and that concern the management and use of drinkable springs that were the property of the Agrarian Association up until today...the so called 'civic uses' and...but why talk to you about these things...it's enough for you to know that it would be great for my mineral water bottling business. And try to be polite. We're also expecting the mayor of the town that has the springs I'm interested in."

"Yes, yes, I understand. The usual story. You lavish the payola and the wads of cash, the politicians in turn pocket them thinking that they'll be rich forever. Instead, the only one who ever really gets rich is you. Where are you going to put your spigots this time?"

"If everything goes well, as it will, I'll take you to the Sibillini Mountains National Park, Montegallo. But now be quiet, the Senator is coming back."

Ascoli Piceno
The Dungeons of the Forte Malatesta
Friday, June 15, 20XX
11:09PM

The stairway seemed endless. The steps carved into rock sinking ever deeper underground, ever steeper and narrower. Morgana Bucci was scared. She really didn't know why she had accepted this invitation—an invitation received three days earlier by way of an elegant ticket left for her at the cash register of the best stocked bookstore in the center of town. The salesgirl had delivered it to her when she had gone to pick up a book on palm reading she had ordered a month before. The girl claimed not to know the person who had left it. The contents had to remain a secret, so much so that the ticket itself provided the instructions for how it must be destroyed. The ritual was familiar to Signora Bucci, given her training and passions.

Morgana Bucci was a beautiful and fascinating lady, fifty years old, an expert in astrology, fortune telling, palm reading, and in general, everything esoteric. While occupying herself over time with paranormal phenomena, she had—in spite of herself at first, then with a consciousness of her gift—discovered that she possessed an uncommon intuition, a sort of sixth sense, which she had never boasted about and which she had never sought to profit from.

"You must consider yourself one of the chosen. After a long and attentive observation, your particular capacity and competence has fully convinced us. Therefore, in a special way we count on your presence at the ceremony on Friday..." read a part of the short missive, which provided as well the hour and address of the meeting. All of which was signed by the "Brotherhood of the Oracles." She had never heard of them. The address was that of the ancient medieval prison of Ascoli Piceno, Forte Malatesta, which she knew to be town property and which had been closed for renovation for many years. She had accepted, pulled along by the irresistible curiosity that had always drawn her to investigate the worlds of magic and mystery. Probably whoever had sent her the invitation knew this and had in fact counted on her curiosity. Now she regretted how easy it must be to read her.

She descended the stairs accompanied by an impassive young woman with very black hair gathered at the nape of her neck; although dressed in a chaste dark grey suit she was clearly accustomed to inspiring admiration for her beauty. Morgana had arrived as instructed at the locked gate of the staging area used by the restoration crews. At that hour it was deserted. She had rung a bell found next to a temporary electrical box. When the black-haired attendant opened the back door it triggered the automatic gate opener.

Little by little as she descended she felt the temperature fall and the humidity rise. The stairs ended. The young woman sped ahead of her and turned down a long narrow corridor. At the end of the corridor Morgana glimpsed a flash of light.

Voices could be heard. She felt—who knows why—a sense of gentle relief. Finally she reached the huge room. Carved into the rock, it was without a doubt deep in the bowels of the fortress. About a hundred people were present, but the strange thing was that she didn't know anybody and nobody took any notice of her. Usually in Ascoli, for better or worse, you run into someone you already know. Instead, on this occasion, she had the sensation of finding herself amidst people who had materialized here for the first time. This odd sensation lingered in her consciousness.

The room was illuminated by an endless number of candles and torches, all white; a huge stone table was positioned at the back, a sort of alter behind which a fresco hung on the wall, perhaps removed from another site and remounted here.

She studied it with attention. Two feminine figures, similar but not the same, almost superimposed with a transparent effect—as if in the act of transformation—rose above a mountain landscape. One held in her hand a sheaf of wheat, the other poured water from a pitcher. Both rested their free hand on the mountain below.

They were beautiful and unsettling.

Advancing through the crowd, she reached the center of the room, where a big stone with strange signs carved into its surface towered. All eyes were directed towards the stone.

She remained perplexed.

Everyone there was wearing normal clothing, elegant, yes, but normal. But what did she expect, a hooded procession ready to sacrifice a virgin and then copulate in a total liberating orgy? She smiled, surrendering to the foolishness of the idea.

At that moment a person made his entrance dressed like a member of the Ku Klux Klan, in a white tunic and hood. Around his neck hung a medallion, the same one—she only noticed this now—that everyone wore. Incised on it was an open book. One of the two pages showed a pitcher with water flowing from it; the other, a sheaf of wheat.

The hooded one began to speak in a deep and resounding voice, amplified by the fine acoustics of the hall, perhaps originally conceived as a place of assembly.

"Dear brothers, dear sisters, tonight we celebrate a special event, an event that is for us a saving grace, seeing the grave danger we are facing. A nefarious occurrence divined by way of our rituals, but which, together with a terrible omen, has also announced—as you remember—the arrival of a knight of noble spirit, ready to fight for the survival of our Brotherhood. Well then, dear brothers and sisters, in this night of the propitious moon, the chosen one is presented to us. Forward, have him enter!"

Everyone turned towards a small door, almost invisible, that opened in a corner of the room.

The announced hero of the evening made his entrance. He was dressed exactly the same way as the person who introduced him, except for the color. His outfit was entirely black.

The man who seemed to be the high priest made the chosen one kneel in front of the stone and then seized his left hand and sliced the index finger with a blade. Making sounds incomprehensible to unaccustomed ears, he guided him in the writing—with his own blood—of the words that Morgana, even though she couldn't make them out exactly at that distance, knew to perfection.

The words were an ancient oath instilling the desire for revenge.

She couldn't be mistaken. Not her, Morgana Bucci. Her ears were too attuned to the sounds uttered by him who everyone—as she had already noted—called Master.

"Now the chosen one is ready," continued the Master. "In the upcoming nights he will act according to his own will, but in our interest. He will stop the sacrilege. The sacred waters will be saved. The Sacred Spring will continue to gush. The traitor to this earth will be punished, and the usurper will be thrown out. Go and complete your mission!"

He who had received the imprimatur of the assembly exited from the scene threading through the followers until he reached the little door through which he had entered. The Master ended the gathering with an announcement that there would be another in the near future. The members would learn of it by whatever means would be held to be most opportune. Before finally dismissing them, he reminded the onlookers of the duty of secrecy sanctioned by the sacred bond of the Brotherhood.

For the first time since she'd entered this subterranean place, Morgana asked herself why she was here. Who had invited her? But, above all, why? She was not part of the Brotherhood of the Oracles and not even an initiate.

Just as she was reflecting on the anomalies of the situation, she felt a hand on her back and it was now that she realized that everyone was looking at her.

Behind her was the Master. He spoke without removing his hood.

"You are asking why, aren't you? Your presence gives me great pleasure, but I must also ask that you keep our secret." The voice was unnatural, modified like an actor doing a bad parody of elevated speech. "I know that you will not make me regret having invited you. You will be invited the next time as well, and if you do not wish to accept, I will understand. In any case, keep the secret."

Morgana stiffened, but hadn't lost control: "None the less, you haven't answered me, although you admit that you've guessed my question. Why am I here?"

A shadow of strong disappointment crossed the gaze of the Master. This gaze was the hooded face's only window of expression, and Morgana saw it distinctly. It was a clear sign that the lord of the house was not used to being contradicted. He repressed it in an instant, sign of a proven capacity to dominate temperamental mood swings.

He replied in a calming tone, "Why not? You are a true

luminary in the field of esoteric rituals. For the Brotherhood of the Oracles you could be a great resource. Til next time."

There was no time for debate. The Master turned and left, followed by a crowd of onlookers begging for an audience without receiving any satisfaction.

No one took any further interest in Signora Bucci. Reluctantly she retraced her way, climbing the stairs in a state of mind very different from that with which she had descended. Not fear, but a terrible curiosity: What vendetta must the chosen one carry out? What danger threatened the Brotherhood of the Oracles? But above all, who was the Master?

Rome
The Piazza of the Pantheon
Bathroom in a Bar
Friday, June 15, 20XX
11:30 PM

Senator Cecchini verified that he had four bars on his cell phone. He already knew that when he found himself in a dead zone, he could always count on getting a signal in the bathroom of this bar. Satisfied with the power of his Nokia, he entered by memory the number of Fabiano Assergi, mayor of Montegallo.

Assergi answered immediately. "Hi Senator, I'm on my way. I couldn't find any parking."

"But couldn't you get a taxi? Hurry! Forlan and I are waiting for you."

"I took my car because I have to leave right away. I've got company."

"The usual crap, huh? Ha ha ha. That dog of a teacher, isn't that so?"

"Are you crazy? If it came out...if we were overheard..."

"But everybody already knows the preschool teacher has been your lover for years."

"Yes, but my wife still doesn't, or my children, so let's drop it."

Senator Cecchini glanced at his watch and after noticing in

the mirror that his nose hairs were growing out, returned to thinking about business. "Okay, don't worry. Listen: when the question comes up, we have to confirm that there aren't any problems and that in the town council meeting on Monday, they will turn over the concession of all the springs of drinkable water in Montegallo to Acque Sane, Forlan's company, for an unlimited time."

"I've told you not to talk about these things on the telephone, maybe..."

"And I tell you again not to worry. Both of us have SIM cards bought abroad, so they can't be tapped. So do you understand me?"

"Of course, And you don't have to explain everything again. The only thing is that if it's for an unlimited time that means it's going to cost a lot more. It will be very hard for me to explain the benefits of making an agreement without limits. It's true that the creation of two plants for bottling mineral water represents the chance to create jobs, but the lack of an expiration date raises a lot of questions."

The Senator was about to lose his patience. More than one person had noted a certain resemblance between him and the mayor, and this really irritated him. Re-examining his reflection in the mirror, he responded bluntly. "The effort will be amply repaid, and you know that. Do you think it's been easy for me to change a law that has existed for centuries? Taking authority away from the Agrarian Association and making it pass into the complete purview of the villages has stirred up a great deal of discontent. Luckily, the bugaboo of the depopulation of the mountain zones has satisfied public opinion, and in any case, as often happens in Italy, memory doesn't live long, or at least not long enough to reveal the truth. Where are you?"

"I've parked. I'm coming on foot. The usual bar, right?"

"The usual. By the way, try to keep that humanoid of the female sex that follows you around, that so-called woman, quiet. Silvio Forlan is a high class person and his companion is even more so. I don't want to look like shit, or to give them the idea that I have anything to do with dummies. Hurry!"

He hung up so that he didn't have to listen to the response. He realized he needed to take a pee. He chose a stall, unzipped his fly, pulled out the necessary equipment and relaxed. A few seconds later he felt the vibration of his cellphone, which he had deposited in the left pocket of his pants. It was the mayor. He answered without interrupting what he had begun.

"It's me. I want some advice."

"Make it quick."

"To look good, what should we order to drink?"

"Two idiots on ice!"

Aggravated, he hung up and put his cellphone back in his pocket, then recomposed himself. He sheathed his sword, pulled up his zipper looking overhead, adjusted his jacket looking down, and then cursed. He had pissed on his shoe.

Montegallo
Upper Bar
Saturday, June 16, 20XX
4:46 PM

"Busso!"

Cesarone played the card, rapping his knuckles on the table and looking into the eyes of his partner Gualtiero, seeking a sign of approval.

He found only a shake of his head, clear expression to the contrary. This was confirmed in the next two plays, in which the opposing pair of adversaries manifested their superiority.

"You ass. You're just an ass. You're just a freaking ass and that's all," Gualtiero said in his thick local accent.

"Don't let it get to you, Gualtiè, we're just better than you, ha ha ha. Drag your belly over to the bar and order us some drinks!"

It was Francesco talking, who, along with Antonio, had just won the daily contest of briscola and tressette. Ritual appointment with Elena, the owner of the upper bar, called "upper" because of its location on the upper piazza, or actually, at the top of the incline, which — if you followed in the opposite direction — took you to the lower piazza, with its own bar called "lower."

Pure logic of Montegallo.

Gualtiero didn't swallow the defeat. "But what the hell are you saying? If this ass here hadn't fucked up, no way you would've won!"

"Now you're just busting my balls! I never get any good cards when you deal... you bring bad luck!"

"Oh so I bring bad luck? When I deal we lose, when I don't deal we lose... you're just an ass!"

Antonio distributed four glasses of white wine and the controversy died down.

"Drink! Drink! Drink! And to hell with anyone who wants to make you drink water!"

The four raised their glasses breaking out in a roar of laughter.

At the corner table, silent and engaged in solitaire, accompanied by the usual Peroni beer, sat the owner of the eponymous woodcutting business, Anselmo Grossi. He broke his silence.

"It's gonna be our ass if the water in Montegallo becomes like wine and beer. The world turned upside down. You'll see when you pay for water like for wine. The same water that pours from the faucet for free now. Ha ha ha! The same, ha ha ha!"

Cesarone: "He's right. The mayor's gonna give away all the water in Montegallo to that guy from Milan."

Gualtiero: "He ain't from Milan, he's from Venice. His name is Forlan. He's a businessman famous for mineral water."

Francesco: "Tain't happened yet. They're deciding on Monday, at the town council."

Antonio: "It's already done. It's done. It's done. We're gonna have to pay for our own water. What a total ripoff!"

Little by little, as time passed, the bar filled up with the regulars. Elena served up coffee, wine, and beer. Giorgio Zappa and Serafino Giuseppucci, both ex-mayors of Montegallo, came in with Domenico Pisana, retired stonemason. The first to jump into the discussion was Giuseppucci. "It'll be a great opportunity for the village, though. The jobs they're going to create will give families the possibility of staying here, and it'll stop the continuous depopulation that we've suffered up 'til now. The employment..."

"It's a disgrace! Giving away our resources to the first comer, without any competition, without asking any guarantees for the future!" Giorgio Zappa countered, immediately interrupted by an unstoppable crescendo of voices that overlapped trying to win out by way of an ever greater level of volume.

After five minutes the chaos was total.

Suddenly, silence.

Silvio Forlan's two assistants had entered. They had made their first appearance two weeks ago in a black BMW X5. Their names were Francesco and Ian. The first, called Checco, was from Rome, the second was Serbian. They had been sent to this place by their boss to make an on the spot inspection. After the first reaction of simple curiosity which they had stirred up in the small mountain community, the two were watched with great mistrust.

They clearly weren't technicians.

Their behavior was much closer to that of two bouncers, and above all, it wasn't clear what inspections had been done up to this point. Actually there was one inspection that everyone was talking about, that is, the one conducted by the Roman in order to see the bed of the owner of the "upper bar." Mere gossip, but Elena was still a beautiful woman, notwithstanding her forty-five years and a life passed behind the counter. Checco represented a new masculine presence with a pleasing appearance and an engaging Roman likability, full of witty banter. Nothing bashful about him, whether by birth or upbringing—he was from the best school of social relations, the Roman suburb of Quadraro.

Ian, on the other hand, was taciturn with a suspicious appearance. His face was furrowed with two scars, one that went from his left ear to the left corner of his mouth, scoring his left cheek, giving his face an altogether sinister expression. The other—as if one wasn't enough—had eliminated just about all of his right eyebrow, deforming the outline of his eye.

Perhaps his silence was an attitude he had developed gradually, as poor Ian grew tired of scaring people even if he was only asking them for the time.

"Good evening everybody! Have we interrupted something? Please carry on." Checco had understood what the subject of the conversation was, but he liked to needle people.

"Maybe we're not supposed to listen...right, Elena?" commented Ian, leaning up against the wood bar and turning his back on everybody.

After a few seconds casual conversation resumed, subdued, but above all, not touching on any water issues.

It goes without saying that a forbidden subject becomes an obsession. The eyes of everyone present, apparently locked with those of their companions, darted away ever more frequently, trying to fathom the attitudes of the two outsiders. One contemplated the foam clinging to the side of his glass, the other flirted with Elena, perched behind the cash register. For the future entertainment of the gossips, the lady seemed to enjoy it.

"But who are those two?"

Domenico Pisana broke the standoff by pointing at the glass door through which two cars could be seen. Two individuals stepped out, one from a Volvo station wagon, the other from an Alfa Spider.

Montegallo
Piazza Francesco Bonelli
Saturday, June 16, 20XX
5:02 PM

"What a meal! You never told me that behind that old bar on the curve there was such a great trattoria. What's the name of the village?"

"Ca`netra or Canètra, I've never really understood. Anyway, it's the best place in the province."

"That's not saying much. I don't care much for the Sabine district. Just olive trees and cicadas. You gotta admit, this zone doesn't seem all that welcoming either."

"Well as far as highways, skyscrapers, and malls are concerned, they haven't really gotten it together yet."

"For heaven's sake, I agree that the natural beauty is extraordinary here. I hadn't remembered it like this. Plus I really do need to relax. By the way, where's your house? We're there, right?"

"Just a little farther, a few kilometers. We're in the main town, Balzo. My house is in Astorara. Excuse me, but don't you remember? This is Elena's bar."

"Ah yes, the red head. Yeah, I remember her. But this isn't the main piazza."

"No. The piazza with the city hall is down there. This is piazza Bonelli, but for everyone here it's the upper piazza. Listen, do you want coffee?"

Saying this Maurizio headed for the entrance of the bar.

Tony was about to follow him, but stopped just in time. A colossal mastodon of a black truck came speeding through the town, barreling down the street between the piazza and the bar.

"What the fuck! He was going to run me down! Did you see that? He almost ran over me!"

"All right, let's go."

Tony succeeded in crossing and they entered the bar.

They felt all eyes on them. For the little community of bar customers, the regulars, this new couple represented a further and irresistible point of curiosity.

"Hi everybody, how's it going?"

Tony greeted everyone there as if they should recognize him. A classic actor's ploy. Usually, in Rome, there would always be someone who did recognize him. This time there was no such response, just a few grunts of welcome.

"Aah, but you're Maurizio, the son of Guido and Milena. How are you?" Gualtiero got up and hugged Maurizio. "It's been a long time! How's your Mamma? We never see you."

The handshakes that followed were sincere. The same hands pulled them down to sit at the table which, up until a few minutes ago, had been a battlefield on which pitiless card sharks faced off. Now it provided support for the unmistakable peace cups. Five rounds of drinks followed. At the sixth, Tony was trying for the hundredth time to tell a story from the world of theater, but for the hundredth time, he was ignored. Everybody was paying attention to Maurizio. This time he was interrupted by Domenico Pisana who pointed at the glass door, "Hey, here comes the mayor!"

"What are you, the doorman? Elena, you'll have to get him a

nice uniform. It shouldn't cost much. How tall are you, Domenico, five feet give or take a couple inches? See, Elena, you'll save money on fabric, ha ha ha!"

The general laughter was widespread. Only the object of the kidding didn't take part.

Fabiano Assergi entered right in the middle of the laughter. "Hello everybody! Having a good time? Especially since your mayor has been looking out for you. A round of drinks for all!" Then, noticing Ian and Checco, "How's your work going, are you satisfied?"

And he went off to the side with them.

Having survived unharmed the umpteenth round of drinks, Maurizio went to greet and thank the first citizen; he also introduced Tony.

After a few idle words, the mania of showing off his role got the upper hand of the local politician. "Guys, I understood immediately that you are men of the world and if you want to go down to Ascoli Piceno this evening, there's a great party that I've been invited to. I'd really like it if you'd join me there. It's at the famous Caffe Meletti in the Piazza del Popolo. Say that you're with me, I'll expect you."

Tony was excited about the invitation, but didn't say anything. Maurizio, who was completely indifferent, thanked the mayor just to be polite.

Meanwhile the bar had filled up with customers: a dozen young people twenty to thirty years old went back and forth between the tables and the bar. The wine and beer gave way to Campari and prosecco. Tony left the seniors and turned to the juniors. He hoped that by changing his public the fascination of his monologues would win greater admiration. On their part, the youth rendered vain this hope. After half an hour, in fact, they began to disperse, with various excuses, and he was left alone. Maurizio was sitting at a table with Anselmo Grossi, the woodcutter, who was accompanied by his cousin Giuseppe Grossi. The woodcutter and Maurizio were old friends, but as often happens, life, or in this case, distance, comes between people. For Anselmo and Maurizio, however, the differences weren't acute. On the contrary, the sanguine and blunt character of the woodcutter had always gotten along well with the subtle irony and the reserved personality of the archivist. They resumed the pleasure of being together.

Tony rejoined them for a few minutes but it was time to go. They hadn't yet set foot in the house. They had to unload their luggage, and luckily for them, they both held their liquor pretty well. It had been a challenging afternoon.

Exiting, they savored the temperature of the sunset in Montegallo, so different from the Roman twilight.

"Follow me. We're going just a little further up, but pay attention, because it's all curves and the road is narrow."

"Not a problem. I'm in great form. In fact, I'd like to go to that party tonight. What do you say?"

"Whatever you want, but why? Don't you like the scene here?"

"I don't know yet. They all seem nice enough, to tell the truth, but I don't know if they like me. I'd like to check out the alternatives. That would make me feel better."

"If that's what you want..."

Ascoli Piceno
Caffè Meletti
Saturday June 16, 20XX
10:55 PM

Count Augusto Piloni de Castris carried out the role of lord of the manor with aristocratic aplomb. The party in the noted Ascoli cafe had been organized by the titled host to celebrate the new wine produced by his family vineyard, Piloni de Castris.

The cream of Piceno high society was there — or at least those who considered themselves as such — as well as the usual party crashers.

The count greeted the mayor of Montegallo and his wife Marianna warmly.

Even though that afternoon Fabiano had shown off the invitation he had received, he was amazed by all this attention. He had never been part of the elite of the city, although he had always wanted to be. Now, finally, he had succeeded and he wasn't very interested in why. He was tired of being the folkloric expression of the politics of Ascoli, the institutional benchwarmer, seated only at tables for those who didn't count, more like part of the meal than a dining companion. And the votes of the mountain zone certainly didn't represent a majority. Remembering Tony and Maurizio, he hoped they wouldn't show up. It might be embarrassing if they used his name to get in. He had invited them so he could look big, not so much to them but to the Montegallo folks who were listening — if they could see him now! However, he didn't really feel at ease. This wasn't his scene, and that made him even more nervous, adding to his discomfort, dragging him down in an infinite spiral of anxiety.

He had met the Count Piloni de Castris only a couple of times and he'd never been greeted like this, at least as far as he could recall. While he was absorbed in this thought, the Count was kissing Marianna's hand, after which he absent-mindedly took hold of Fabiano's. Well! "I'm very happy that you're here, Mayor, and that you've come too, Signora Marianna."

"Thank you, Count, always such a gentleman. My husband was in a big rush to get here but I explained to him that important people make the others wait a little. Not too long, just enough so they notice your absence."

"Marianna, quit talking nonsense. Count, thank you so much for the invitation, we'll leave you to your other guests. Come, Marianna, let's go drink a little champagne."

"At my parties one drinks only wine. My wine. Good evening." The Count moved off, raising his most classic eyebrows.

The mayor tried to digest his glaring gaffe.

A vibration in his pants pocket pulled him out of these dark thoughts. An SMS. He saw immediately who had sent it.

"Problems back home?" Signora Assergi asked apprehensively.

Problems, yes, but not at home, and Fabiano couldn't let on where. "No, no, everything's fine. Excuse me, I'm going outside for a second. I have to make a call and it's too noisy here. A political matter."

"But don't you use the other phone for work? The one they can't tap?"

"Be quiet! I told you to never talk about that phone! Besides, that's only for a few people. Most of my colleagues have my old number. Wait for me here, near the bar. I'll be right back."

He made his way through the other guests until he reached the entrance manned by the security guards, who let him out while holding at bay a conspicuous knot of supplicants wanting to attend the event. He moved off to the side, staying under the portico facing the Piazza del Popolo, and dialed a number that wasn't in the phone's memory, but was very clear in his.

"What were you thinking? I told you not to ever send me messages. At the very most, call me on an anonymous phone, but never leave a message."

"You took her to the VIP party! Bastard! You never even told me about this evening at the Meletti. You coward! Everybody in Montegallo knows about it except me!"

"I didn't tell you about it because I didn't want to make you mad. Come on now, calm down. I swear that you'll forgive me. But now I have to go back inside."

"Go ahead, go! I want to see how you're going to make this up to me."

"Listen to me ... we'll see each other tonight at the usual place. My wife is staying in Ascoli. I'll tell her that I have an obligation early tomorrow morning, so I'll spend the night up in Montegallo, okay?"

"Okay, but if you're screwing with me I'll make you pay."

"I swear it, honey. You'll see, I'll give you a nice present, understand? Do you understand? Hello? Hello?" The mayor snorted. Luckily, Michela Angeletti had already hung up.

Ascoli Piceno
Piazza del Popolo
Entrance to the Caffè Meletti
Saturday June 16, 20XX
11:20 PM

"Good evening, we have been invited..."

"Good evening. Could you tell me your names please?

"Maurizio Verdimani and Tony Liberati, but probably..."

"I'm sorry, but you aren't on the list. I can't allow you to go in."

"I know, but like I was trying to tell you, we were invited at the last minute by the mayor of Montegallo and..."

"I'm sorry, but there must be some mistake. This party was organized by Count Piloni de Castris. You can't come in, you aren't on the list."

"Yes, I'm aware that we aren't on the list—at least I suspected as much—but, as I saying, there's a reason..."

"I'm sorry, you aren't on the list and I can't let you in. Could you step aside please? You're blocking the entrance."

"If you could ask inside, maybe ask the Count...what did you say his name is?"

The situation was becoming embarrassing. Tony was getting stubborn, the security guard was getting nervous, Maurizio was ashamed. "Tony, let it go. Let's leave, what do you care about these waxworks?"

"But excuse me, why? The mayor said we could enter using his name, I don't believe that...Mauri, what's the mayor's name?"

"Gentlemen, it seems to me that you're a bit confused. You don't know the name of the Count who organized the party, you don't know the name of the mayor who you claim invited you. I've been patient, now leave."

"But how dare you? I'm calling the person in charge."

"I am the person in charge. And you can't go in."

"Tony, I'm fed up. Let's go."

Maurizio was losing his patience, something that didn't happen often. On the contrary, it was normal for Tony to flare up over nothing and then forget about it five minutes later. But not Maurizio.

"Tony, I'm really getting pissed off. Drop it. We'll go somewhere else, besides it's hot."

"That's why they invented air-conditioning. But now, it's a question of respect. Get me the Count."

"The Count is not to be disturbed. I ask you for the last time to leave, otherwise I'll be obliged to..."

"To what? Obliged to do what? What are you going to do? What do you want to do?"

Tony Liberati was 6ft 2in tall, weighed over 220 lbs, and was regularly victimized by his own ego. Once this was called into play, it unleashed a sort of Mister Hyde, otherwise he would never hurt a fly. Maurizio knew him well and knew the conflict underway would not find an easy solution.

Suddenly, a voice arose from the corner. To be exact, the corner to the left of the entry way.

"I swear it, honey, you'll see. I'll give you a nice present, understand? Do you understand? Hello? Hello?"

Maurizio recognized the voice immediately, and also immediately saw a way out.

"Mayor! Mayor! Excuse me..."

At this point the mayor couldn't turn back. If he didn't get them inside, he would lose face before all of Montegallo. The two would tell the story with terrible consequences for his image. So he went inside and asked the Count if he could introduce two friends who had just arrived from Rome—one of whom was a successful theater actor. Augusto Piloni di Castris, although annoyed, was most polite. He went back to the entrance and welcomed Tony and Maurizio as much awaited guests.

Tony, his beautiful victory made clear, not only didn't take his revenge, but even gave his regards to the security guard.

Maurizio intuited right away the true state of the Count's soul, and decided to consider it unbearable, but he too had the good manners to fake it. Besides, there was a strange coincidence here. Physically the two resembled each other very much, except for the bald pate which characterized Augusto Piloni di Castri. Both were

tall and very thin, with an elegant comportment. The lower part of
each face was bordered by a finely trimmed black beard ending at
the chin in a sharp well-modeled point. To complete the irony of
fate, both of them were wearing a bow tie wrapped around a long
slender neck.

Next to these three, Fabiano Assergi looked like a genetic ex-
periment that had turned out badly: short, pudgy, with bug eyes
that protruded more than they should have behind a pair of glasses
with round lenses.

They all went inside.

The Count returned to the two women he had left in order to
resolve the dispute outside.

The mayor returned to his own lady, who was gulping down
her fourth glass of wine.

The two friends, once they were over the threshold, stopped to
look around. Then Tony leaned in close to Maurizio's ear, partly to
overcome the volume of the music, partly to be sure no one could
overhear him. "You know something, Mauri? The Count looks a lot
like you."

"What are you saying? He's bald."

"You'll be bald too, but look at the beautiful women surrounding him."

"Oh all right. Let's go get something to drink."

Ascoli Piceno
Caffè Meletti
Saturday June 16, 20XX
11:45 PM

The beautiful women Tony referred to were Giulia Cantarini, reporter for the local edition of the daily newspaper *Il Messaggero*, and
Morgana Bucci, noted Ascolana scholar of the occult.

Giulia Cantarini was there, above all, for work. In the Monday
edition of the Roman daily — the most read in the Piceno zone — the
regional insert for Le Marche would amply cover the party. The
article would mention the Count's wine, the real star of the evening.

Therefore Signora Cantarini was treated with maximum respect. A prime opportunity for free publicity depended on her. Certainly it couldn't be said that this was the peak of her journalistic career. More to her taste, she had just published an article on the not-yet-completed restoration of the medieval prison, the Forte Malatesta, describing her tour of the site. Although she was tired of being a flack, perfectionism overruled her frustration. Even on this occasion she tried to do her best. Every so often she snapped a few photos or took notes, and then returned to blend in with the beautiful people, glass in hand.

Tony was immediately attracted to the journalist. She was an intriguing woman, with a fascinating demeanor of natural detachment as she participated in this parody of the dolce vita, of the select evening amongst the provincial VIPs, of the "I would like to — but I can't — be the famous billionaire Briatore."

Also feeling out of place was Morgana Bucci. She was not interested in aspiring to, and even less in reaching, the social finish line. She had decided to come only because she didn't believe in coincidences. It was the second unexpected invitation in two days, but while the first one might have made a certain amount of sense, this last one was hard to understand. She already knew the Count. An unpleasant and haughty man — at least that's how he had always seemed — who this evening, contrary to every expectation, was acting affable and hospitable.

Luckily she had run into Giulia, a close friend even though ten years younger. They had been stationed at the bar for half an hour when the Count came over to thank them for coming and to offer them something to drink. It was a great honor to welcome the famous Morgana Bucci, he had said. This declaration of esteem surprised both of them. Both would have expected these words directed at Guilia Cantarini, chronicler of the event underway. Instead the head of the house had immediately betrayed a particular interest in Morgana. But perhaps fearing that he was going too far, he had decided to momentarily abandon the two ladies, leaving them in the company of two glasses of Piloni de Castris red wine.

"You've made quite a conquest, eh? Good going, Morgana!"

"How good remains to be seen. He makes me nervous. There's something disturbing in his way of operating."

"In my opinion he's very elegant and has a certain savior-faire. You should be more appreciative of his attentions."

"Look at those two instead. They're not bad, a bit bohemian for this affair, but not bad. With any luck, they aren't even from Ascoli."

"Let's go and ask."

"But no, wait. Where are you going?"

"Curiosity is feminine, right?"

Saying that, Guilia walked smiling towards Tony and Maurizio, who, for their part, were planted in the opposite corner under a large mirror.

The movement did not escape the actor's notice. On the other hand the trajectory traced by this body, not exactly heavenly but curvaceous enough, resembling Charlotte Rampling's double, was followed by most of the male eyes present in the cafe.

It was noted that the goal of this short diagonal walk was represented by those two strange types, one with the air of someone who had seen better places, the other with, "Look, here I am!" written all over his face.

"Now hell's bells, I really am going good tonight!"

"Going where?"

"Nowhere. It's a way of saying that I'm in top form. Don't you see that one coming towards me?"

"Towards us."

Rome
Via Cassia
Villa Araba Fenice
Saturday June 16, 20XX
11.:55PM

Silvio Forlan handed Senator Cecchini a pocket mirror and a short silver straw. On the reflecting surface, four lines of white powder; on the side the thumb of Forlan, who was doing his best not to cut himself with the razor blade.

Emidio accepted the offering. His awkwardness revealed his status of neophyte in the many levels of cokehead. With difficulty he straightened himself up from his sprawled position on a black leather couch, elegant like all the furniture in the place. The Villa Araba Fenice had been put at Forlan's disposal for a very private party, in which the guest of honor was precisely himself, the Senator.

Two seminude girls helped pull him up in a triple maneuver, supporting him physically on either side, pampering his ego with lascivious caresses, and showing him how to use the straw, necessary conduit between nostrils and cocaine.

Forlan, for his part, threw himself into lavishing attention on the other two professional entertainers, specialists in lightening the existence of rich personalities already wearied of sparing no expense just to forget the daily routine for a few hours. Conducting these special guests on the voyage of pleasure at the Villa Araba Fenice was Lady T, a Sicilian trans with a breath-taking body, including an additional option of more than ten inches for those who love the "sandwich." Lady T excelled above all in the demi-monde of prostitution because of her refined tastes and her capacity to satisfy the whims of her clients whatever those might be.

For the moment the Senator contented himself with banal transgressions, avidly snorting the fourth line of coke. At first he'd been afraid, and had only gone along so as not to look bad in front of his friend Silvio. But now he had to admit that he liked it, especially since it was accompanied by top-of-the-line Champagne. He felt euphoric, capable of enjoying to the depths the joys that life could offer him and which, up 'til now, he had not fully plumbed.

The time had come to let it all go, to harvest the fruits of a political career cultivated in the shadow of the Roman clique that headed up the Party. Enough with prudence, enough with scraping together the crumbs left in a ridiculously small quantity sufficient only to feed the political ambitions of a provincial politician. Time to raise his sights.

And to take another snort.

Had to aim for higher targets. And if this didn't mean a bigger role at a higher level of power, too bad. There was still the money, you could shoot for that, and Forlan — the king of mineral water — presented a great opportunity in that sense.

"So, dear Silvio, everything is set for Monday. The town council will grant the concession for the utilization of all the springs of drinkable water present in the territory of Montegallo, for an indeterminate amount of time, to your company Acque Sane. A toast!"

"We'll make that toast after the meeting on Monday. I'm superstitious about business. I can't confess this to Simona because she'd bust my balls with positive and negative influences, astral conjunctions, and various energies, but even I believe in it a little bit. So just make sure that brain dead mayor sticks to our agreements. They've already cost me enough."

"No problem. He's convinced that he'll look good to the voters, seeing how many jobs the bottling plants will provide."

"There aren't going to be any jobs."

"What?"

"I said there aren't going to be any jobs."

"But what are you saying? How are the two bottling plants going to function? And how are you going to justify the incentives that you're putting in place? You can't expect to get financing without giving guarantees of productivity!"

"Listen up, Senator. The tax break that I'm getting will serve to build two completely automatic bottling plants. The necessary personnel will consist of six technicians who already work for me, transferred in from another one of my plants. The maintenance of the system will be entrusted to a French company, and the trucking contract let out to a carrier from Rieti. I don't want any of those dickhead mountain men under my feet. Is that clear?"

"Yeah sure, it's all clear. But I'm warning you this could make big trouble with the people there."

"And you know how much I give a shit? Plus, if you want to know everything, after five years the plants will be shut down, goodbye and thanks."

And they each took another snort.

"Okay, you won't have any problems. The important thing is that you hold up your end of the bargain." Having said this, the Senator returned to the pleasures provided by Marika and Ludmilla. In short order, he found himself frolicking around the room completely naked, excited like a satyr at his first bacchanalia but...there was something that wasn't working.

His member was far from responding to the stimuli that his possessed brain was sending in that direction. It had the aspect of a tired snail.

And to think that he had never even seen a tired snail.

Ascoli Piceno
Caffè Meletti
Sunday June 17, 20XX
12:05 AM

Giulia introduced the two guys to Morgana right away.

Tony was flying high. His ego was soaring aloft and then plunging headlong towards the derriere of the journalist. He strutted like a peacock, made jokes, told tall tales. Basically, he laid out a tremendous line of bullshit.

Maurizio showed the attitude of a true gentleman. He smiled with embarrassment at his friend's performance and refilled the ladies' glasses, counterbalancing the conversation in form as well as content. Every now and then, however, a shadow crossed his gaze. Moments in which he darkened, absenting himself mentally to a place known only to him.

Moments, only moments.

He was forced by events to interrupt these flights.

In the course of an hour Tony had gulped down three bottles of Rosso Piceno.

In full euphoria he jumped up on a table and improvised a rather audacious piece of cabaret, targeting two well-jeweled elderly women. The onlookers were aghast. Only Giulia and Morgana seemed to be entertained; Tony noticed this. Going too far, he lowered his pants, turned his back, and at the peak of his frenzy, showed his hairy buttocks to the ancient victims of the jest.

Pandemonium broke out.

The security forces intervened. Four bouncers seized the unfortunate ham who, with dropped britches, lost his balance and tumbled to the ground.

The four encircled him.

Maurizio, worried for the fate of his friend, threw himself into the fray.

Irritated by the ignoble spectacle, the Count Piloni de Castris entered the scene, obviously to calm the spirits—already derailed—of the vulgar intruders and the useless plebians who had been entrusted with the task of keeping watch over the party.

Tony, grabbed from behind, made a standing jump with his pants rolled around his calves. Maurizio twirled around throwing punches without hitting any target up until the moment when the Count chose to intervene physically. He had seen that his words, even though spoken in his noble voice, were producing no effect.

Unaccustomed to barroom brawls, poor Augusto tried to separate the fighters by checking the impetus of a bodyguard. This gave Maurizio the opportunity to free his right, which was dodged by his expert adversary and ended its flight on the cheekbone of the peacemaker.

The Count fell to the wood floor. The thud that followed, in conjunction with the importance of the protagonist, achieved a conciliatory effect.

Everyone calmed down at once and did what they could to help their host.

In a corner, Tony tried to regain his composure, pulling up his pants, while Maurizio went to ascertain the condition of the Count who, in the meantime, had stood up. He appeared to be all right.

Turning to Maurizio, he pronounced a single phrase before returning to his guests. "Please leave the premises immediately."

Maurizio and Tony were escorted outside by the security guards.

They found themselves facing each other, silent and confused, and then they both let fly.

"You're a dickhead! We made total asses of ourselves. You got it?"

"But what about you? You punched the Count! You got that?"

Laughter from beyond broke up their tete-a-tete. Giulia and Morgana were satisfied spectators of the unexpected events.

"Girls, are you tired of that wax museum?"

In the course of the next five minutes the four of them strolled across the white travertine pavement of the Piazza del Popolo, glistening after a violent thunderstorm that had just finished hammering the city.

"We need something strong. Let's go get a drink at a place I know." Giulia said this.

"Oh Mauri, this is the woman of my dreams!"

They all laughed

An hour later they said their goodbyes.

At 2:30 AM Tony and Maurizio were coming up on the last curve in the direction of Piazza Taliani. Each was driving his own car, Maurizio with a smile stamped on his face. There wasn't a specific reason, just that the evening had turned out to be very enjoyable thanks to the presence of the two ladies. Companionship experienced in a straightforward way, without the frustration of a dutiful courtship or the hysterical search for a conquest. One of the things that made him laugh even more was remembering the story Giulia told about a stone phallus on the top of the bell tower of the Church of San Francesco, placed there by masons who hadn't been paid by the monks who administered the church. He was astonished when Morgana pointed it out to him. She explained however that the story of the masons was wrong. The carving represented a pre-Christian symbol — later adopted, in rare cases, also by Christianity — relating to a male god. In fact, there *was* a phallus rising up on the north bell tower, perfectly visible from the Piazza del Popolo. He was truly entertained.

The exact opposite of what had befallen poor Tony. He had struggled the whole time to come off as interesting, especially to the journalist, for whom he had unsheathed his usual brilliant eloquence, the infallible vehicle of the fascination which he presumed to command. Signora Cantarini, while much amused, had not fallen into the arms of the capricious ham, pushing him away at the moment when he had made a clumsy move in the vicinity of her lips.

Wounded ego. Sacrilege!

Having passed through Balzo, the administrative center of Montegallo, the two automobiles began to climb the slopes of Mt. Vettore. Tony's Alfa took off, attacking turn after turn, revving the motor that responded with a roar at every shift of the gears. Maurizio followed calmly. Not slowly, but with the measured coolness that characterized the way he did everything. He watched the flashes of the high beams of the car ahead of him; in the dark the double reds of Tony Liberati's taillights drew the jagged course of the asphalt on the flank of the mountain.

Suddenly another set of headlights burst through the dark, a car coming from the opposite direction at high speed. Their paths crossed at the next curve.

Maurizio turned off the radio and lowered the window. In the silence of the night the screech of the brakes sounded sinister, like the scratching of a fork on a porcelain plate. At that moment Tony's fast and nervous progress was abruptly interrupted. The lights of the Spider remained fixed, illuminating a small portion of the woods while those of the vehicle that he had just encountered continued on until they passed Maurizio, who had pulled over onto the narrow edge. He was able to clearly make out a black BMW X5 tearing off in an unbridled race to who knows where. Getting back on the road, in two minutes he found his friend on foot on the shoulder, white as a ghost, scared to death but unhurt. The right side panel had suffered some damage, given that the car had ended up half off the road, but the damage was only to the body. This was confirmed by the ease with which the starter did its duty.

Tony drove with the adrenaline that again coursed through his nervous system blurring his reflexes. Luckily, the journey was brief. He entered the house mouthing a phrase over and over like a lullaby. After a few minutes he regained control by placating his nerves with two glasses of vodka, but he continued to repeat at the top of his lungs the same question.

"Who the fuck was that?"

Montegallo
Church of Santa Maria in Pantano
Sunday June 17, 20XX
10:30 AM

The two forest rangers were making their usual rounds. Marco and Paolo had worked for years at the National Forestry Office in Montegallo. In the summer their zone filled up with tourists and an almost constant presence was necessary in the part of the communal land that lay within the Sibillini Mountains National Park. The forest rangers were also essential in case of any public emergencies. The Comune (or Township) of Montegallo, in fact, even though it was quite extensive, had only five troopers under the command of Marshal Francesco Moser. This last, sharing the same name as the great cyclist, lived in Balzo with his family, next to the station of the Carabinieri, Italy's elite paramilitary police force.

The six forest rangers played a decisive role in the control of the territory, which consisted in large part of a mountainous environmental preserve and was mostly uninhabited. Around five hundred residents were distributed in the twenty villages.

In the summer, and the spring and fall weekends, the human presence increased dramatically, boosted by the arrival of tourists, hikers, mushroom hunters, nature lovers and environmentalists. Experts and novices of the mountains who, like ants, mingled on the provincial roads, village alleys, dirt paths, mule tracks, and trails of every type with the goal of reaching a meadow, a wood, a stream, or even a pull-off where they could spread the table cloth for a picnic and an outdoor jaunt. Or, a restaurant. But also hunters, given that the other part of the territory was outside of the park, whose borders ran right through communal lands. The contiguity of the two zones led to a strong presence of game in the part where hunting was permitted, provoking a certain amount of crowding during hunting season.

On the contrary, in the winter—or during the week in other seasons—even the five hundred residents abandoned the country to live in the city. Only at the beginning of summer did a conspicuous number return and remain for all of July and August. But that wasn't enough to justify an increase in the forces of order, which was always understaffed and had to make extraordinary efforts during the so-called "high" season.

This Sunday in June was a very "high" day.

Marco was the first to step down from the green Panda 4X4. He stretched, yawning—he had already been on his feet working for five hours. He took a deep breath to fill his lungs, enjoying the place and the moment.

In front of him was the church of Santa Maria in Pantano. Solitary and mysterious, sitting at 1200 meters in altitude on the slopes of Mt. Vettore, it had watched over these mountains since 740 AD, having miraculously survived an avalanche that at one time swept away the adjacent monastery.

The field facing the little entrance portico, usually an inviting oasis for tired hikers, was deserted this morning. Maybe because it was still early. Marco and Paulo's service vehicle was the only jarring note in the harmony and peace of the place. Above, the deep blue of the sky; all around, green triumphant in every shade and silence inhabited only by the voices of nature: birds and insects busy and heedless of the presence of humans, while wild boar, foxes, and deer hid themselves in the woods, mistrustful of the only mammal capable of messing up this paradise.

Because this was a paradise.

Now Paolo got out of the auto too and stretched. He went over to the far side of the field to the left of the portico, unbuttoned his fly and enjoyed a good piss in the open.

"Aaaaah!!!" PRRRRRR. He farted. "What a sight!" he added.

After he buttoned himself up, he lit a cigarette and set himself to looking at the thousand year old stones of Santa Maria in Pantano, also called Santa Maria delle Sibille. This church had been here in the middle of the woods for 1200 years, five kilometers from the closest village of Astorara.

While his thoughts were wandering, following the fissures between the blocks of stone of the ancient "tetris," he noticed that the wooden door, usually barred, was showing a crack that was a little bit too wide.

"Hey Marco! Come over here for a second."

"What's up?"

"Look at the door."

"What about the door?"

"It isn't closed right. It isn't tight against the wall like usual."

"Let's go look."

"They might've done an inspection for the restoration of the frescoes."

"The restoration has been finished for a while now and further work isn't expected."

"Maybe the parish priest came to get something."

"What do you mean, there isn't anything in there anymore."

"Then maybe it's some shithead vandal."

"Get the flashlight from the car. There's no electricity for the lights."

Marco went to look for the flashlight. Paulo approached the door. He gave it a little push and it opened with a screech, letting fly a fistful of dust into the air.

"Here, I found it."

They entered, throwing the door wide open. The light that filtered in from outside succeeded in illuminating only a few feet. The back remained in the dark.

The room was very large, but empty. Dust was the only furnishing, distributed in a uniform layer on the pavement.

With the flashlight they could find the door on the opposite wall, on the right. It was closed from inside, easy to open. This time the light revealed the other half of the room, showing the recently restored frescoes. They floated magically on the three back walls, representing sacred figures like the Madonna and Baby Jesus along with the Sibyls, feminine divinities of pagan origin, a strange mixture of primordial Christianity and ancient popular traditions.

On the wall opposite this last opened door, on the sides of the vault that met the ceiling, the Sibyls Agrippa and Ellespontica appeared, lit by the rays of the sun. In the center, an image of the Nativity; lower down, between the prophets Jeremiah and David, the Annunciation. But between the kneeling Madonna and the Archangel Gabriel, there was something that shouldn't have been there.

Written in a red that was clearer than all the rest, in block letters.

"THE WATER IS SACRED."

Below the writing a face. The expression was contorted, the gaze without life. All of this, however, in three dimensions.

"What the hell!"

"It's Angeletti! The teacher!"

Michela Angeletti was seated on the floor with her back against the wall, her legs extended and her feet bound with metal wire. Her arms behind her back. On the ground, a pool of blood. On her body, a pool of blood. On her neck, at the base of her throat, the source of all the blood.

Montegallo
Village of Astorara
Sunday June 17, 20XX
11:40 AM

"But where are you going?"

"Mauri, I told you. I'm leaving, going back to Rome." With his duffel bag slung over his shoulder, Tony headed for his car parked in the little town square of Astorara, in front of the old fountain once used as the drinking trough for cows and sheep.

Maurizio, in the doorway of his renovated house, tried to dissuade him, without, however, following him. It seemed he didn't want to separate himself from these stones.

"Wait! We'll leave tonight! Look what a beautiful day it is!"

"Listen, I understand you. You like this place. You've been coming here a long time, you know everybody and everybody knows you. But I don't give a fuck about it! They all give me weird looks. If I make a joke nobody laughs, if I don't drink with them they get offended but if I offer a round nobody accepts."

"It's not like that. That's just your impression. And them, them who? They aren't all the same. If you observe these people closely, you'll discover a lot of good things about them. Anyway it isn't like you're forced to go to the bar."

"Oh yeah, right. On the road you're a lot better off. Last night they just about killed me. You saw that too, right?

"I saw that it had nothing to do with you. That jerk was going too fast for his own reasons. He could have run into anyone and he ran into you. How is this village involved?"

"It's involved because, in all these years, such a thing has never happened to me and I've traveled everywhere. In this place everything seems totally bizarre."

"There's nothing bizarre here. You're a superficial egotist, incapable of looking beyond yourself. Just because nobody recognized you? Just because the girls don't give you a second look?" Maurizio got up close and vomited these words in Tony's face.

"That's what you think of me?"

"No, that's what I think of what you've become."

Eye to eye, they stared each other down for a long time. In silence. Until Marshal Moser and the Carabiniere Morini arrived.

"Signor Verdimani?"

"That's me."

"And you are the owner of this automobile?"

Moser was referring to the Spider with the wrecked side panel.

"That car is mine," Tony broke in, "What's the problem?" The aggression of the preceding few minutes lent a testy tone to his question.

"There's more than one. Let me see your license and registration."

"Listen Marshal, we're here on vacation and we're leaving today. Unfortunately, last night, when we were driving back from Ascoli, each in his own car..." Maurizio spoke cautiously. He was trying on the one hand to understand the marshal's line of reasoning, on the other, to head off a fight with his hot-headed friend. "Tony was ahead, and once we'd gone through Balzo...in fact, beyond Collefrate, after the first turn..." The marshal let him talk while looking through the documents. "...a black SUV came down the road at high speed and forced Tony off the road. It didn't slow down at all. I was a few hundred yards behind, and I guessed from that idiot's headlights how fast he was going and pulled over to let him pass. Maybe he didn't even see me, and when right afterwards..."

"Yes, yes, I understand, Signor Verdimani. Now both of you will have to follow me to the station." Moser handed the documents back to Tony and made this announcement without releasing any other information.

"Officer, we were leaving and we're already late. I'm not interested in filing charges." Tony snapped.

"Nevertheless you have to give a statement."

"Come on, Tony, let's go with the marshal. Once we've given our statements, we'll make tracks. Half an hour more or less won't make any difference."

"I'm sorry, but you won't be able to make those tracks. Follow me to the station."

"Are you arresting us?" This time it was Maurizio raising the objection.

"I didn't say that, but after you've made your statement, you'll have to stay here in the village at our disposition."

"I can't stay here. I have to go back to Rome." Tony was falling into the grips of an hysteric attack; Maurizio clearly felt uneasy.

"Gentlemen, above all, calm yourselves. Last night something very serious happened a few kilometers from here, and it is my duty to follow procedure in this case. Therefore, for now, you're going to remain here in Montegallo at my disposition. Let's go."

SECOND PART

Rome
Parioli District
Apartment of Senator Cecchini
Sunday June 17, 20XX
12:45 PM

The telephone had been ringing for a while, but Emidio Cecchini was still in the arms of Morpheus, dreaming of Lady T.

The night he had spent at the Villa Araba Fenice had raised him to the highest peaks of pleasure. Or at least that is what he had thought when he had crawled into bed at six in the morning. Exhausted, excited, exhilarated, confused, drunk, unsure if he would repeat the experience, with a vague sense of guilt . . . and his heart wouldn't stop pounding in his chest. After-effects of cocaine. But once again Lady T had anticipated the problem before letting him leave. She had recommended a few drops of Valium. He had followed the prescription, enjoying the benefits right up until the moment he heard, far away and unreal, the trill of the telephone.

"Hello?"

"Finally! Something terrible has happened up here."

"Hello, who's speaking?" The Senator couldn't breathe well, his nose was clogged.

"It's Fabiano in Montegallo. Hello! Do you hear me?"

"Yes, yes, I can hear you, don't yell." The Senator blew his nose.

"Of course I'm yelling, they killed Michela!"

"What?" The Senator snorted up a hawker.

"Michela Angeletti is dead! They murdered her! What the fuck! Don't you watch the news? Montegallo has been on every channel all morning long."

"I just now woke up, I was out late last night." He grabbed the remote and clicked on SKY TG24, without the sound, and went on talking with the mayor.

"They found her in Santa Maria in Pantano. She was slaughtered like a pig and they wrote on the wall with her blood, 'THE WATER IS SACRED.'"

"Who wrote that?"

"Who knows? Whoever wrote it killed her and the reference is pretty clear to me. Tomorrow I'm cancelling the town meeting and the day's agenda."

"Listen up! You're not going to cancel anything. Postpone it for a week. We need time."

"I don't know. I'm not sure. I'm fucking worried."

"Have they already questioned you?"

"Not yet."

The Senator pulled up another hawker. "Don't say a word without consulting a lawyer. I'll send you one. Don't say anything before he gets there."

"That's no use, I already have a lawyer. I think the Carabinieri are about to arrive."

"Oh! So maybe it really was you who did it?"

"You're insane! Don't say that even as a joke."

The Senator blew his nose. "But what was Michela doing at Santa Maria in Pantano at night?"

"At Santa Maria, I don't know. But she had a date with me at Colle, only I couldn't get away from my wife so I didn't go."

"That's the same area. Maybe someone followed her."

"Yes, but there's going to be a record of the last phone calls between me and Michela."

"That's for sure. In fact, why would you make a night time date at Pantano?"

"Michela was furious. I took my wife to a party at the Meletti, she found out and made a scene over the phone, so to make her forgive me..."

"You're an asshole."

On the television the Senator saw a close up of the mayor, a blurry photo in which his crooked smile seemed more out of place than ever.

The media trap was set. The link between the phrase written by the killer and the concession of the water rights was in the spotlight as well as the relationship between the victim and the mayor. Anything that wasn't already in the public domain would be soon enough. Cecchini chose not to underline this. With somebody as scared as Assergi, there was always the risk of everything going up in smoke. He couldn't allow that.

"I don't need any more grief from you," the mayor replied with a sigh.

"Try to keep calm. Stay with your wife. You should always be seen with her, and convince her, by whatever means, to remain near you. Better still if you release an official statement. Now I have to go. Ciao."

"Wait, I want..." Click.

Emidio Cecchini was still far from his best. He needed to recover his energy. Talking with that idiot hadn't helped, and even less helpful was the situation that had blown up 200 kilometers away, where a complication of this sort had never been dreamed of. He spent the next two hours channel surfing. The news at 1:00 PM, 1:30 PM, 2:00 PM, the news crawl, the updates on the channels dedicated to 24 hour news, all talked about the Crime of Montegallo. All of them, without exception. A place where, up until now, you only ended up if you took the wrong road, was now flooding across the screens of the all Italy.

A blind alley in the heart of the Apennine Mountains in the Marches—an ideal spot for a quiet business deal—had suddenly become the bull's eye of national news.

"Shit! The only thing missing is a plastic model of that talking head, Bruno Vespa."

Provincial Road of Piceno
Direction — Montegallo
Sunday June 17, 20 XX
2:39 PM

The title could be: **The Mystery of the Sibillini.**

Giulia Cantarini was euphoric about the assignment she'd been given.

Il Messaggero had entrusted her with what they were already calling the story of the year: the murder of Michela Angeletti, the pre-school teacher found with her throat slit in the oldest church in Montegallo.

Even better: **Murder on Mt. Vettore**

The journalist drove her car like an automaton towards her destination, wallowing in the expectations of this great occasion. Her gaze, lost in a thousand thoughts, fell on the dashboard clock. She turned on the radio to the 2:30 PM newsbreak, hoping it hadn't ended. They were talking about the crime at that very moment.

"In Montegallo, a small township in the province of Ascoli Piceno, situated within the Sibillini Mountains National Park, the body of Michela Angeletti, fifty-seven years old, has been found. The death has been ruled a homicide. The woman — a pre-school teacher by profession — had her throat slit. The Carabinieri were called in on information provided by two forest rangers. They had found the body inside an isolated church, 1200 meters high on the slopes of Mt. Vettore, during their normal rounds. For now there is no further information. There are no indications regarding the motives or possible suspects. The only clue is a disturbing phrase written on the wall with the victim's blood, 'THE WATER IS SACRED.' Sources yet to be confirmed suggest a relationship between the victim and the mayor of Montegallo, supporter of an initiative that has divided the countryside: the concession of water rights for the numerous local springs to a private concern. More about this in the upcoming editions."

She turned off the radio with a smile on her lips. The case was already of national interest. For sure, she would also be on television. She needed a fantastic headline: **Blood at a High Altitude.**

No, she could do better.

She had answered the phone call from the editor in chief at lunchtime. There was just time to pack bags for herself and her daughter Sara, to leave the child with her grandmother, and to tell her ex-husband to go pick her up later. Now she was at her office gathering together her laptop, two cameras, a tape recorder, a small video camera, the related batteries and chargers, two cellphones with SIM cards from different companies, and finally, her good luck charm.

She loaded everything into her Class A Mercedes, and dashed over to Morgana's.

Her friend was originally from Montegallo — her grandmother was born in the village of Corbara, where the family still had a lovely house. She had been there more than once with Morgana when they were younger, and local family connections could be very useful. But she needed Morgana to accompany her, her presence was indispensable. She explained the situation to Morgana who was totally in the dark — she watched very little TV and she hadn't gone out of her house yet. It wasn't easy to convince her, it took Giulia half an hour to achieve success. Morgana was busy in the afternoon, she was meeting with Count Piloni de Castris, so she would drive up in the evening in her own car. As for the rest, there was no problem — they could stay at her grandmother Caterina's house. The excitement of the new adventure did not stop Giulia from taking note of the unexpected development.

"Congratulations! You didn't let the opportunity slip last night!"

"If you are referring to the Count, let me inform you that it was a total surprise to me, too. This morning he called to invite me to his house this afternoon for coffee. It's strange, like I told you, up until yesterday we had only exchanged the most superficial greetings and platitudes. To tell you the truth, I've never liked him."

"And now, instead?"

"Well, I'm curious. He's a fascinating man, and I'll admit, good looking. So, I decided to go."

"Of course, you did well. The important thing is that you join me tonight. That way, first you can tell me how it went and then you can help me investigate the case."

"Okay, even though I don't understand what I have to do with it."

"You're indispensable, that's all. You know the area, you know lots of the people who live there, you come from a local family. No doubt you can help me gain their trust regarding the whole story."

And what a story! **The Blood Soaked Mountain**

Still not quite right.

Giulia arrived at the Piazza Taliani in Balzo at 2:55 PM.

She found it crowded with people and equipment, vans bearing huge antennae labeled RAI, MEDIASET, SKY, and many other channels, both radio and television. Various groups entered and exited the town hall with the demeanor of people who have not yet solved anything. She catalogued them immediately as colleagues. Others stopped on the opposite terrace, suspended in front of the majesty of Mt. Vettore; almost everybody turned their attention in one direction, towards the slopes of the gigantic rock. The point of interest became immediately clear to the eyes of the reporter, marked as it was by the lit headlights of the vehicles in which the examiners had reached the scene of the crime. Nobody else could get close. A pair of correspondents, with their respective cameramen, were interviewing passersby, in an attempt to learn and broadcast the opinion of the townspeople.

Quick as ever in figuring out the best strategy, she decided that she wouldn't learn anything new here, just what would corroborate the official bulletins. But those were already available.

No. She would go the police station, betting on her powers of persuasion and on getting a chance for a private talk with the commander of the station, Marshal Moser.

It was time to start working on her piece.

Montegallo
Carabinieri Station
Sunday June 17, 20XX
3:24 PM

"This is the third time I've told you what happened, and it's the third time I've told you I didn't see the driver's face. I'm sorry but...you know...I was concentrating on not shitting my pants out of fear."

A smile escaped Marshal Moser. The first since this whole business had started.

For three hours he had been shut up in his office with his colleague, Captain Fianchini of the RIS—the criminology lab of the Carabinieri. In fact the experts had gotten involved immediately. The gravity of the event set in motion the measures prescribed in such cases, amongst which—an important priority—the analysis of possible clues at the scene of the crime.

The next step would be to hear the likely witnesses. In a small place like Montegallo, it didn't take much to know by morning, from the sounds heard during the night, of a probable car wreck. Having determined the zone, the rest had been easy. One of the implicated automobiles was the Alfa Spider of Antonio Liberati—known as Tony—actor by profession, resident of Rome, here in the country as a guest of Signor Verdimani.

Place and time of the accident were both close to that of the crime.

Liberati admitted to the accident right away. He told the same version every time he was asked to repeat it, without ever contradicting himself. While he was confirming for the hundredth time that he hadn't seen the driver's face, a Carabiniere entered the room with a sheaf of papers in his hand. He handed them over to Moser. It was the deposition, signed and probably copied many times, of Maurizio Verdimani, employee of RAI, resident of Rome, owner of the house in Astorara where Liberati was staying. Now Tony was allowed to leave the office of the marshal and took a seat in the waiting room lobby under watchful guard.

After a quick reading, the marshal found his impressions confirmed. They weren't lying. Verdimani's deposition basically repeated his friend's, adding however, two important particulars. The automobile was a black BMW X5, the driver was alone — at least, that is what he seemed to remember — and presumably male.

"What does this mean, 'presumably?' Did he see his face or not?"

"Not well, he says."

"In any case we have a lead. Check out all the black BMW's present in the area."

"Right away, Marshal,"

"Not a word, please. With anybody. There are reporters everywhere. Remember, this is just a starting point, nothing more, it's not verified as the killer's car. Is that clear?"

The official from RIS was in complete agreement, knowing full well from experience how dangerous the uncontrolled spread of news could be. "If the word gets out, every driver of a black X5 will risk a lynching."

"Now go and put out the bulletin, to the forest rangers too. Every vehicle of this description, with the passengers, is to be brought here to the station. Use discretion, please."

At the very moment when the Carabiniere opened the door to leave, Verdimani pushed himself forward. "Excuse me, may we go, or do I have to call my lawyer?"

"Enough! Enough already! I can't take anymore! You better believe we're calling a lawyer. I'm going to the press, to the television. You'll come off looking like shit. This is an abuse of power. We've been locked up for hours describing a simple car accident in which, by the way, I was the victim..." Antonio Liberati could not hold it in any longer and the explosion was beyond his control.

"If you don't calm down right now I really will arrest you." Moser was losing his patience.

"Shut up, Tony, let me talk. So we aren't under arrest?"

"No, not for now."

"So we can go?"

"Yes but you have to remain available to us."

"What does that mean?"

"That means you can't leave Montegallo. Relax and enjoy the view. Pretend it's a vacation. We'll let you know as soon as possible."

"But why? And how long do we have to stay in this hell hole? I didn't do anything and I don't have anything more to say than what I've already told you."

The two commanders, taking their hats from the desk, went to leave without addressing the river of protests from a Liberati ever more hysterical, but then Fianchini stopped at the threshold and turned back to the witnesses: "Gentlemen, not a word with anyone or we'll hold you directly responsible for anything that interferes with the investigation."

Without waiting for a response, the officers closed the door and headed for the building exit.

They were getting into the Subaru that was the service vehicle for the Montegallo station when Francesco Moser was blocked by a beautiful woman who first called him by name and then grabbed him by the arm.

"Marshal, wait. Just a few questions. I'm the correspondent from the *Messaggero...*"

"Signora, for heaven's sake! There will be a press conference in the meeting room at the town hall at 6:oo PM. You'll be given all the information about the case then." Saying this he freed himself from her grip, slammed the door briskly, revved the motor, and sped off, leaving Giulia Cantarini to twist in the wind with her genial investigative strategy. While she was reflecting on her own stupidity, she heard the main door open again. She forgot in an instant the failed approach that she had just attempted and concentrated on a new assault on the scoop of the day.

"And now?" Tony stopped with his head hanging low. The guard had ushered him out with Maurizio who, with much more energy, walked towards the street.

"Now I'm hungry. There's a restaurant in the piazza where you can get a great meal. Maybe with all these people around, it's still open. I'm going there."

Tony felt drained of all energy, but above all, he couldn't drive

out of his mind the argument he'd had with his friend that morning.
"Wait. I want to ask you something...Maurizio!...wait for me!"

The reporter was disappointed not to find herself with a couple of investigators. She artfully hid her disappointment and put on her best smile. In a moment like this the presence of these two at the police station couldn't be coincidental. They surely had something to do with the homicide. But in what way?

"Hey Tony! Ciao! Don't you recognize me? It's Giulia."

"Of course I recognize you, it's just that I didn't expect...but what are you doing here?"

"What are *you* doing here?" she replied cleverly.

"Nothing. Last night, when we were coming back from Ascoli..."

"Tony! Come on, otherwise they'll be closed."

"Okay, I'm coming. I'll see you later. If you want to join us we'll be at the restaurant in the piazza."

In the meantime, Maurizio had gotten the car, turned it around and raced to scoop up the naïve lady killer.

"Are you totally feeble minded? They told us not to say anything."

"But not to say anything about what?"

"I don't know, but something serious must've happened last night and we've been caught in the middle of it."

After they'd gone a hundred meters, they realized that, in fact, something really must have happened. Balzo was full of people.

"Shit!"

"I want to know something...Maurizio, are you listening to me?"

"Yes, yes...tell me."

Maurizio couldn't believe his eyes. He'd never seen so many people in this little town. Only on the day of the August fair, maybe. On foot, in cars, in the two bars, in the Piazza Taliani looking towards the mountain. It took forever to find a parking spot, it would have been better to have left the car in front of the police station. He opened his door to get out, but Tony still hadn't asked him anything. He stopped and looked him in the eye, "Well?"

"Well what?"

"What do you want to know?"

"Ah...yes. Listen, do you really think that I've turned into what you said this morning?"

"Can I ask you something?"

"Of course."

Tony was hanging on his friend's response. He had called him an "egotist." He had called him "superficial." But above all, it was Maurizio who had said these things. Now Tony hoped for a kind word.

"Aren't you hungry?"

Yes he was.

That was the kind word.

Montegallo

Courtyard of the Carabinieri Station

Sunday June 17, 20XX

3:53 PM

There was nothing left to do but wait for 6:00 PM. She looked at the police station and thought that the officers serving in Montegallo were freaking lucky. The place looked like a mountain villa built to enjoy the best views of Vettore and the valley below. Part of the structure consisted of the residence reserved for the marshal and his family.

Giulia Cantarini could make out this division as she examined the side by side entryways. There was a visible difference between the two front yards: bleak and austere on the station's side, a garden overflowing with plants and vases of flowers on Signora Moser's, inhabited at that moment by a chubby little blond yard monster racing around on his tricycle.

"Hi there kid. What's your name?"

The boy stopped in the middle of a slalom between a vase of geraniums and a lemon tree. He stared at the pretty woman without speaking. She was pretty, but he didn't know her, so he couldn't answer.

"Well? You're not going to tell me your name?"

Yes, of course, because she was pretty. "I'm Massimo. And you?"

"Hi Massimo, I'm Giulia."

The curtain on the first floor window moved. After a few seconds the door opened, "Massimo, come in here."

"Wait, Mamma, I have to finish the race. Just past the roses and then I'll come back."

The little pedals creaked, the tricycle set off, and the adventurous young centaur circled his private Eden.

Signora Moser was about to insist, but Giulia sensed a small hesitation. She wasn't going to let the moment escape. "My compliments on your garden, Signora. It's marvelous."

"Thank you. Massimo, come on, do what I tell you."

"Signora, excuse me. I'm waiting for a friend who has a house here in Montegallo. I've arrived a little early, and I need to use the bathroom, but the bars are full of people...I don't know what to do..."

Massimo parked his mighty machine at his mother's feet and, making her bend down, whispered something in her ear.

Then with decisive steps, he went over to the bemused Giulia, took her by the hand, and accompanied her inside the house.

Montegallo
Village of Fonditore
Sunday June 17, 20XX
4:00 PM

"There it is. The black BMW X5." Marshal Moser had immediately thought of the car used by the two technicians from Acque Sane. It was his habit to keep tabs on the people who settled in Montegallo. On the arrival of Ian Vladic and Francesco Baldacci he had checked out their particulars, ascertaining that the two were employed and didn't have any previous criminal records. Vladic, a Serbian national, was also in order regarding his work visa. The automobile they drove was registered in the name of Silvio Forlan's company, this too, completely in order regarding every letter of the law.

The town government had lodged them in two small apartments carved out of what had been at one time an elementary school. The village of Fonditore is located more or less at the center of what the locals called "Infected Valley." The uninviting denomination could be traced back to an epidemic of hoof and mouth disease that had broken out amongst the cows two centuries earlier. In spite of the misleading name this remarkable strip of the territory, in which six of the twenty villages of the zone were located, was charming and luxuriant. Up until the 1970's the high number of residents made the school necessary. Subsequently, because of the depopulation of the entire mountain region, the school was closed and, after decades of disuse, transformed into apartments with the aim of stimulating local tourism. A fiasco, since the structure, not very attractive to the eyes of potential customers, had not achieved the hoped for success. At that point the town administration had decided to use it to handle exceptional situations. The construction of the bottling plant for the waters of Vettore was considered to be one such situation.

Fianchini got out of the Subaru first and knocked on the door of Apartment #2, which Moser had pointed out to him.

"I'm coming! Just a minute."

Ian Vladic took a little too long to open the door. When he did, his appearance was particularly smiling and pleasant. He did the best he could with the face he had. "Ah, good evening. I thought maybe you were Francesco."

The RIS marshal noted the peep hole in the entry door. "You are..." he was consulting the papers in a leather folder.

"Good evening, Ian." Moser had approached as well. "He's Vladic," he then said, turning to his colleague. "Can we come in?"

"Yes, of course. Please make yourselves at home."

Kitchen, bedroom, and bath, small but comfortable.

The first room seemed to be mostly in order, not surprising since the two men always ate at the restaurant. A dirty glass in the sink was the only sign of life.

The criminologist headed into the bedroom.

The bed was unmade. Vladic, who was wearing overalls, had swollen eyes and disheveled hair. He had been sleeping.

On the desk against the wall, a closed laptop, an ashtray full of cigarette butts, an almost empty pack of tissues and a wallet. On the floor, a wastebasket full of used tissues.

Omar Fianchini looked around in search of something that would explain the lapse in time between when he had rung the bell and when the tenant had opened the door. An excessive lapse, it seemed to him. But everything seemed normal. Even the bathroom was clean and orderly enough.

Moser stayed in the kitchen to interrogate the person who, at the moment, could be defined as the only suspect.

"So, Ian, you were telling me that after 11 PM last night you didn't leave the house again?"

"Exactly. I was working all night on the computer. I went to bed this morning around ten and just now you woke me up."

"Vladic," the marshal switched from first to last name, "Last night around 2:30 AM a car was forced off the road by a black BMW X5. If it's true what you're saying, our technicians can confirm it by analyzing the on board computer of your car parked out front here."

"What do you mean parked out front?" Ian Vladic seemed sincerely surprised. And he seemed even more so after he went to take an incredulous look and came back inside to try to give an explanation.

"Marshal, Francesco took the car last night after he'd dropped me off, but then he never came back. He had an appointment, and I thought he'd spent the night out. But he probably returned the car so that I wouldn't be left on foot."

"Who did he have an appointment with?"

"That I don't know."

"With a man or a woman? For what reason?"

"I don't know! I mind my own business."

"Where was this appointment?"

"I don't know. I didn't ask. We have a very limited relationship. The only thing we share is work. The rest is private."

The story might stand up, but then why was he so nervous?

It was obvious he was hiding something. "Signor Vladic, we have to ask you to hand over your car and your laptop." The marshal became ever more formal.

"Okay, if there's no other choice...but I need the laptop for work. How long are you going to keep it?"

"As long as necessary, and you'll also have to help us locate your colleague, Francesco Baldacci, understand?

"No problem, I'll call him now. Can I get my cellphone?"

With a nod of agreement Marshal Moser accompanied him into the other room. What he saw there surprised him quite a bit.

The RIS investigator was coiled under the desk reconnoitering the right corner near the wall with latex gloves. It took a few minutes for him to reemerge. He had a little cylinder in his hand. Without taking notice of the two spectators, he started to tap it vertically on the table top, then he unrolled it: a ten euro banknote. Tapping it again on the wood edgewise, he turned to his colleague.

"Come and look."

After a quick glance, the two marshals turned to stare at Ian Vladic.

"Are we taking any bets that it's cocaine?"

"You now, come with us. The apartment must be searched. We're going to give this place an extra good going over, if you can't give us the exact information regarding the identity and place of the appointment with Baldacci. If that's even a true story."

"I don't know anything about that stuff. That banknote has probably been there since who knows when. Plus you're dealing with crumbs. I told you the truth, I've been here since yesterday evening."

"Then you won't have any problems taking a drug test. At least to reassure your employer and the town authorities who are hosting you."

The tension of the moment transformed poor Ian's face into a portrait by Picasso. The two scars traced the furrows of a violent past which he'd succeeded in leaving behind. He had reached his current level thanks to Silvio Forlan. Ever since he'd been hired by the king of mineral waters, while he might find himself involved in shady situations, he had achieved a new life thanks to his employer.

However, his mentor required absolute prudence in private life, nothing that would interfere with business activities.

"Okay, okay, I'll tell you everything I know, but I beg you to close an eye to this part of the story. There's no more coke in the house. I had less than a gram, and I used it to stay awake."

"You're that dedicated to your job, Signor Vladic? What was so important that you were working on it all night?"

"It wasn't for work. I was playing Poker on the internet. If you check my laptop, you'll see that's the truth. I connect to the site through my cellphone and bet with a credit card."

Moser assessed the Slav's version; it might make sense. In any case, he had to uncover the rest. "Where's Baldacci?"

"I don't know!"

"Let's go. You'll have to come with us to the hospital for the drug test."

"I can't do that."

"Ian, don't piss me off. There's been a murder, so try not to make an even bigger mess of your situation."

"A murder? Who?"

Fianchini took advantage of Vladic's bewilderment. "Who did your colleague have a date with?"

"He said it was with Elena, the barista," Ian answered with a sigh of resignation.

Moser and Fianchini exchanged a look. "Keep going," they said in unison.

"Yesterday afternoon we were in the bar, and I saw Francesco talking with Elena for several minutes. I was at the counter, he was next to the cash register. I couldn't hear what they were saying, but when we left he was all revved up. He told me that they were going to meet up around midnight."

"Where?"

"Francesco made it clear that both the time and the place had to be kept secret... I'm not sure but... I'd never heard of it before. The name of the place was maybe 'le pianette,' 'le pianelle,' 'le...'"

"'Le pianelle,' yes, in the Pantano area." This fired up Moser's interest.

"When we separated after dinner, that was the last time I saw him. Usually I can tell when he comes home. He's next door and his bathroom is on the other side of the wall from my kitchen. But last night I didn't hear anything. Still, I wasn't worried. I thought he'd convinced Elena to go back to her house or to a hotel. I didn't even hear the car."

Vladic paused, but Moser's sixth sense as a detective had been awakened. For the most part, he'd gotten what he'd been hoping for. "Go on."

"That's all, I swear."

"Ian, don't give me the run around."

"For now that's fine. Come with us to the station for a deposition," Fianchini intervened. "Find yourself a place to sleep, but don't leave town. The apartment has to be searched and the car too. Follow us."

"Can I call Francesco?"

"You'll have to. In fact, let's do that right away. Give me your cellphone and tell us the number,"

The RIS officer punched in the number that Ian recited.

"Either it's turned off, or it's unreachable."

Montegallo
Piazza Taliani
Ristorante La Locanda del Cacciatore
Sunday June 17, 20XX
4:30 PM

Mixed antipasto with prosciutto, homemade soft pork sausage, wild boar salami and assorted cheeses. A sampling of Castelluccio lentils. A little bowl of organ meats. Pappardelle with wild rabbit sauce. Wild boar stew with porcini mushrooms. Zuppa Inglese.

Tony and Maurizio ate everything, talking the whole time about only one thing. In the little restaurant they made sense of the day, wasted despite themselves in the long interrogation with the two marshals.

Thanks above all to their hostess, Signora Lorella, with her smile fixed as if paralyzed and her constant stock phrase, every eight minutes — "Everything okay?" She and her husband, the cook with a passion for hunting, had told them all the details of the murder at Santa Maria in Pantano.

The room was filled with about thirty customers distributed around the wooden tables, on the wooden chairs, on the wooden benches, within the four wood paneled walls, in front of an (obviously) wood-burning oven. Everybody was talking about the same thing.

It was the fourth turn of the tables for lunch on an extraordinary Sunday. Between journalists, TV correspondents, technicians and the simply curious, around two hundred guests had come through the doors.

Anticipation focused on the press conference announced for 6:00 PM in the conference room at the town hall. The time was whiled away at a seductive dining table spread with the most disparate of fantastical main courses, taken from the oven with the hypocritical concern and underground enjoyment of table companions transformed into cooks of an unknown reality. The devouring chefs served up hypotheses in sauce, exchanged opinions with truffles, conceived theories of lamb.

While emptying glasses of Rosso Piceno and Passerina wine.

Everyone in Montegallo knew the victim, but the most enjoyable dish set before the avid chatterers was the sweet and sour taste of the adultery between the victim and the mayor, Fabiano Assergi.

The bloody writing had drawn attention to this last character, and to the actions expected on the following day regarding the concessions to Forlan's Acque Sane. The community was divided in two: those in favor who saw the operation as an opportunity for economic development; those against who believed it to be an attack on local autonomy and patrimony.

From there, the public opinion's most widespread conjectures revolved around whether the author of the crime was a local. Someone who, feeling cheated out of a right consolidated over the centuries, had lost his head and sent a message that was ultimately over the top. This scenario was favored because it opened up infinite possibilities for gossip.

The list of suspects was the entire local census.

Others, however, spoke of a crime of passion. They fantasized about a "first lady" assassin, or more directly about a murderous mayor, who, to ward off suspicions, had turned attention towards the political question so as to pass himself off as the object of intimidation. The most far flung hypothesis was that Michela Angeletti had killed herself for love, but the level of lucidity of those who followed this line of reasoning was inversely proportional to the level of alcohol in their blood.

In an hour Tony and Maurizio had acquired every known particular regarding the murder of the preschool teacher, but they took great care not to tell anyone that they had furnished the only serious clue to the investigators.

Lorella was serving their coffee when Giulia Cantarini made her entrance. "Hey guys, can I join you?" Without waiting for an answer she sat herself down at the table with the two Romans, giving each of them a kiss on the cheek. "What were you two doing over at the police station?"

Suddenly there was total silence.

The voices hushed. The glasses stopped clinking. The entire restaurant went quiet. Everyone turned to stare at them in hopes of enlightenment.

In the seconds that followed, Maurizio couldn't resist the temptation. He took a breath and "BROOOT!"

A record belch.

Tony shot a quick glance at his friend, who had become all at once the center of the universe—or at least, of this microcosm—and burst out laughing. Giulia imitated him, followed by all those present. The diversion was successful. The reporter, taking advantage of the light moment, dropped the subject at once to avoid the possible recurrence of interest. "Who would've thought? I haven't been to Montegallo since I was twenty years old. By the way, Morgana's coming later. She has a house here, her grandmother was from Montegallo, so I asked her to keep me company."

"In what sense?" Verdimani tried to regain his composure.

"In the sense that since I have to stay here for some days on behalf of my newspaper, I asked her to help me with the investigation."

"We've also decided to stay here for a while." Liberati glimpsed a new opportunity. The refusal of the previous evening had left its mark.

Giulia grabbed the ball on the bounce. "I'd like to think that you two could give me a hand as well. Let's make a team!"

"Of course! It would be our pleasure. Right Maurizio?"

"Oh, why not? None of it seems real to me."

Giulia Cantarini began to whisper, inviting the two to get closer. "But what were you doing with the Carabinieri?"

Montegallo
Piazza Bonelli
Home of Signora Elena
Sunday June 17, 20XX
4:52 PM

Moser and Fianchini waited for Elena in the company of her father. The commander of the Montegallo police station preferred to interrogate the bar owner at her own home. He didn't want to make things difficult for her, at least not now.

Finally she arrived.

"What's going on? Papa, would you go to the bar, please? I don't have anyone to take over for me."

"Yes, but..."

"Go on, Signor Maggi, don't worry. Everything's all right." Moser reassured Alberto Maggi, encouraging him to leave so he didn't have to make the request himself.

Left to themselves, Fianchini took the lead, and, in order to determine the veracity of Vladic's version, went straight to the point. He wanted to check the Elena's reaction.

Elena confirmed everything. She candidly admitted she'd had no intention of going, but by stringing the guy along, she kept two good customers.

Francesco Moser believed her; he knew her well. She was a good person, but everything took second place to her commercial interests.

Her deposition, while consistent, resolved nothing. In fact it didn't clear Francesco Balduci, who remained the prime suspect.

The only person present at the place, at the time, of the crime.

Ascoli Piceno
Villa Piloni de Castris
Sunday June 17, 20XX
5:17 PM

The clattering of the teaspoon, tapping the sides of the cup of coffee poured by the Count himself, constituted the only sound in the surreal silence, the fruit of a momentary impasse in a stuttering conversation.

Augusto Piloni di Castris had received Morgana Bucci in a living room very different from what she had imagined.

The furnishings were basic: two huge chrome bookcases; a rectangular plexiglass table surrounded by six chairs of the same material, a white leather couch set at an angle; a high tech mobile bar; a 46" LCD TV with a DVD player and Dolby surround sound.

She had pictured a dark and dusty ambience full of antique furniture collected with Baroque taste. But there was no trace of red velvet or gold leaf. On the other hand, the building itself had already proved Signora Bucci's imaginings wrong.

The Count's villa arose in a residential zone of relatively recent construction—the 1970's, to judge by the architectural style. Nothing like the medieval palace with tiny windows, groaning doors, and suits of armour guarding frescoed salons, which she had been expecting to visit. She definitely wasn't expecting to find herself in front of the four enormous glass cases located on the longest side of the room.

Inside each one was a snake.

Morgana wasn't able to relax; she was distracted by the reptiles. The Count had received her very cordially and had seated her in this room without mentioning their singular presence.

At the beginning she had tried to act like it was nothing, but—intensified by the lord of the manor's dark eyes, with which she wasn't able to hold steady contact—the feeling of discomfort became unbearable.

"Count, I can't help myself, may I ask you a question?"

"I've asked you to call me Augusto, and not to be so formal. Unless that's a problem."

"It's not a problem provided that you reciprocate."

"Of course, Morgana, what is it?"

"Okay, I'd like to know...those snakes?"

Augusto Piloni di Castris exhibited a kindly smile framed by a carefully tended goatee, relaxed his shoulders as if finding comfort in a question he'd feared would be more difficult, and rose to his feet.

About 6'3" tall, wearing a beige linen suit, he headed for the reptile tanks, giving the impression of sliding smoothly across the floor. His thin build sketched the elegant line of the Ascolano aristocrat. His shaved head was set on a slender neck, placed in turn on two broad shoulders. Seen from behind, it gave the impression of a rugby ball mounted on a neck painted by Modigliani.

Once in front of the tanks he stopped and turned, like a circus ringmaster announcing the next number. "This one is Kurgan, a royal python, this one is Messalina, a female boa constrictor. This one is Yago, an Indian cobra, and lastly this is Emidio, an example of the Orsini viper."

"Orsini?"

"Exactly. It's named after the zoologist from Ascoli who was the first to describe and catalogue it."

"Is he dangerous?"

"Quite. But like the rest of his dimensions, his teeth are also rather small, and the amount of poison he can inject is similarly low, usually insufficient to do serious harm."

"The other three belong to well-known species, but this one I don't really know. Where did Signor Orsini find him?" Morgana asked, joining the Count to better observe the four reptiles.

"Dear lady, this little ophidian is found in Italy, only in the Appenines of Abruzzo, Umbria and Le Marche, at an altitude above 1000 meters. I believe our fellow citizen had the opportunity to observe him right here in our mountains, the Sibillini."

Morgana began to walk along the wall, pausing for several seconds in front of each tank. During her walk, with her gaze always fixed on the serpents, she decided to express what she was really thinking.

"Count..."

"Augusto! Please, call me Augusto."

"No, for now I'll call you 'Count.' Maybe later I'll call you Augusto. Tell me why you wanted to meet with me. Why did you invite me to the party? For years, up until last night, we've never exchanged more than the most casual of greetings. What has changed?" As she spoke the last words she fixed him with her eyes.

Her companion showed no reaction, and without moving an eyebrow came closer to his guest. "To tell the truth, I don't know." Then he turned and continued to speak while pacing the length of the room. "Last night's invitation had no specific reason. I wasn't even involved with the guest list, the marketing office of my business took care of that. They invited all the important people who live in the city."

"Then why did you have me come here today?

"Because last evening I talked with you. I had a chance to listen to you and watch you. And I became curious about you, one might even say fascinated. Please, accept my friendship."

Morgana was thrown by this explanation, simple to the point of seeming sincere.

"Augusto, I don't know what to say, maybe I've been rude, please excuse me."

"There is nothing to excuse."

"Yes, there is. Forgive me again. But unfortunately, I have to leave now. Starting tonight I'm going to be spending the next few days in Montegallo."

"In Montegallo?"

"Yes, I promised Giulia Cantarini I'd keep her company while she investigates of the case of the murdered teacher. I have a family home in one of the villages there, we'll stay for several days."

"Is it a big house?"

"Pretty big. Why?"

"I hope you don't think I'm being too forward, but can I ask a favor of you? Could you take me along for a vacation in Montegallo?"

Morgana's jaw dropped. The Count took advantage of this and went on, "I want to take a few days off, but I don't want to go just anywhere and so, why not visit my native land?"

"Why not? That's fine."

"Good. You go home. Give me half an hour to get ready and I'll come pick you up."

"Okay. I live at..."

"I know where you live."

The Count produced one of his calm smiles, then took her to the door and said goodbye.

Left alone he went into the garden, entered a shed and emerged with a fluffy white rabbit. Caressing it, he reentered the living room and went over to Messalina.

"Children, I'll see you in a few days. Be good, I urge you."

He stopped petting the little animal and set it in the boa's tank.

"Buon appetito!"

Montegallo
Piazza Taliani
Town Hall Council Room
Sunday June 17, 20XX
5:55PM

The airless room was too small to contain the packed crowd of journalists and technicians. Giulia Cantarini was accompanied by Tony and Maurizio. She had successfully passed them off as her collaborators, since the controls put in place by the sole official of the municipal police weren't enforced with much severity.

Maurizio yanked on Tony's arm and spoke into his ear, trying to keep his voice low. It was perfectly obvious how upset he was. "Listen, I'm going to leave. I can't face staying here. I'm going to the bar."

"Wait, there's only five minutes left. Aren't you curious to know..."

"Tony, I came here to relax, to enjoy the place the way I've always known it, tranquil, silent, peaceful. Instead, I find myself in hell."

"I like all this activity. Maybe I'll get an idea for a play. You know, when something happens you have to ride the wave, plus all the national TV stations are here, which might be useful for me."

"You're all crazy."

Maurizio started to go but Giulia — unaware of his discomfort because she was concentrating so hard on the movements in the back of the room — turned to him like a little girl visiting Disneyland. "Look! Look! There's the major of the Carabinieri, Giorgio Baracca, and the substitute prosecutor, Paolucci."

Maurizio didn't have the courage to dampen the enthusiasm of the journalist, whose euphoria was similar to that of a Rolling Stones fan encountering Mick Jagger and Keith Richards. He decided to stay a few more minutes. Out of the corner of his eye he saw Tony laughing under his mustache.

At the center of a rectangular table, where the mayor of Montegallo usually presided, sat the officials and the magistrate; on either side, Marshal Fianchini and Marshal Moser; standing behind them, Fabiano Assergi with his wife and the entire council and the Secretary General of the community.

Suddenly the banks of floodlights lit up, positioned for the best shots by the TV crews. The heat became more oppressive, the air even more unbreathable. The buzz, up until now uninterrupted, ceased. Major Baracca spoke first.

"Ladies and gentlemen, I am here to give you the official statement relative to the investigation into the murder of Michela Angeletti. At the end of the statement the press conference will be considered finished, that is, no questions. As you know, this morning during their normal rounds two forest rangers found the lifeless body of Michela Angeletti inside the church of Santa Maria in Pantano. The cause of death was loss of blood. The wound, made by a sharp instrument, was inflicted at the base of the throat with the technique usually used by farmers to slaughter pigs. The weapon employed — with all probability, a knife with a blade at least ten inches long — was inserted and driven longitudinally downwards until it grazed the heart. The blade severed the arteries with great precision, thus causing the loss of blood. The body was propped up against a wall that bore writing traced with the blood of the victim. This is presumed to be a message from the killer. I'm speaking in the singular because the one clue recovered by the RIS technicians so far permits us to hypothesize the presence of only one person at the scene of the crime. We have in fact gathered a single type of footprint, other than those of the victim and the two rangers. The clearness of the tracks is due to the thick layer of dust present on the pavement of the building, the residue of recent restoration work. Furthermore, thanks to the statements collected and the investigation developed by Marshals Moser and Fianchini, we are looking for a certain person who seems to have been in the area at the time of the crime. We take this opportunity to thank the agents of the State Forest Service who continue to assist the investigative work carried out by the Carabinieri."

Giulia was rapidly taking notes, and had also turned on her tape recorder. Tony followed along with an open mouth. Maurizio was sweating, restless, cursing under his breath.

Baracca went on.

"For this reason we are pursuing our inquiries across the entire local territory and in the neighboring communities..."

Maurizio elbowed his way to the exit and headed down the corridor that led to the stairs. On the front step he distinguished the voice of the correspondent from TG3 asking confirmation regarding the content of the writing left by the killer. There was no way to make out the rest. Once he was outside the voices he heard were too many and too confused to allow any association with the familiar faces on the small screen. An incoherent and inconclusive concert in which the only distinguishable words were "water" and "mayor."

He could give a shit.

Looking at the mountain, the clouds that bedecked it and the forests that clothed it, he stretched, yawning, and decided...

To enter the bar and order an anisetta on ice.

He took the glass and went outside. He seated himself at one of the tables in the small portion of the piazza that was marked off by rectangular planters, facing Mt. Vettore.

Someone surprised him with a slap on the back. "The vacation is over!"

"It hasn't even started." Maurizio recognized the speaker—

Anselmo Grossi, the woodcutter and his companion in innumerable summer escapades. An intelligent personality educated only by instinct and experience, a rare demonstration of how school desks are not indispensable to success in a profession, nor in the attainment of a maturity that, willy-nilly, life often ends up requiring.

Anselmo got a beer and sat down to watch the sun set too.

"A classic." These were the only words spoken for a quarter of an hour.

The silence was broken by the excited voices of two Carabinieri talking back and forth as they got out of their cruiser and started to run towards town hall. "They found him! They found him!"

"Where?"

"We don't know. They say at the Mount... or on the Mount... or something like that."

"But who found him?"

"The forest rangers again."

"So they arrested him. Great!"

"What do you mean? They found him dead!"

"He killed himself?"

"No. Somebody killed him."

Not a minute passed before a rumbling crowd flooded out of the doorway of the town hall.

Tony and Giulia were among the first to free themselves from the embrace of the same foul air which had held Maurizio hostage. He hailed them. "Hey! I'm over here. Come and have a drink."

Trailing behind Tony, Giulia couldn't stop complaining, cursing those who had interrupted the press conference. "But why? Why? Who knows what's happened. Because something must have happened... as soon as those two Carabinieri came in and whispered something to the Major, they shut everything down. Maybe they found him."

"Of course, of course. What would you like to drink?" Tony's interest in the investigation had vanished the moment his mouth had become unbearably dry. For him the interruption was a liberation.

"Do you want to know what's happened? I know."

"Don't jerk me around, Maurizio, I'm already mad as hell."

"I'm not jerking you around." He recounted what he'd heard.

"So they found the suspect but, if I understand you right, he's good and dead."

"I don't know if it's the suspect, but whoever they found is definitely dead, and they also said he'd been killed."

"And what does it mean, 'on the Mount'?"

"It means 'on the Mount'."

"What?" Only now did Giulia become aware of Anselmo's presence.

"On the Mount, or, like we say, 'u Monte.' The Mount is where Montegallo was originally settled. If you want I'll take you there."

"Let's go."

Giulia got up, dragging Tony by the arm.

Anselmo headed for his pickup.

Maurizio followed them swearing.

Montegallo
The Mount
Sunday June 17, 20XX
7:12 PM

They had just left the town behind them when Anselmo's pickup turned off the asphalt road and climbed up a dirt trail. On the summit of the Mount they could see the emergency vehicles, although this time their lights were out so as not to attract the attention of the journalists and the curious.

At the peak of the hilltop stood the transmission tower that distributed the signal for the entire territory. Who knows what could be seen from up high... Montegallo and all of its villages spread like a sunburst around this promontory...

Maurizio, in all these years, had never climbed up there.

His imagination set to work.

He thought about an old book he'd read as a kid, which contained, besides the story of Beato Marco, various historical essays concerning the origins of Balzo.

Up until the middle of the sixteenth century, the castle of

Santa Maria in Gallo stood on the Mount, from which came the name Montegallo. Later on the inhabitants settled lower down, giving life to the original nucleus of the current town of Balzo. After 1500 the zone probably experienced a certain political and social stability. The demands of war and defense had diminished, giving the population the option of moving to a part of the territory that was more hospitable from the climatic point of view. The houses had been built downhill using the stones from the castle, from its walls, from the churches and dwellings that it had protected.

When they had almost reached the summit, Maurizio, Tony, Giulia, and Anselmo realized that they couldn't go all the way to the top in the truck. They had to stop short. The scene of the crime was isolated and well supervised.

Anselmo knew this place like the back of his hand. As a boy he had gone there hunting foxes in order to sell their pelts. He suggested they go the rest of the way on foot.

The voices of the officials could be heard close by. The woodcutter told his companions to follow him in silence. The unusual quartet began to climb in single file, circling around their goal. Anselmo picked out a path and they made their way upwards through the underbrush.

In silence they moved branches, avoided blackberry bushes, placed their feet where the leader put his.

Anselmo remembered the times in his youth when he had combed the area with his gun over his shoulder, without a hunting license.

Giulia looked around trying to memorize the setting so she could reconstruct it in the piece she would write that evening.

Tony thought that a bar, or at least a kiosk, where you could get a gin and tonic would really be great.

Maurizio imagined the life in this place before 1500. He remembered that the book he had read as a boy had described the dimensions of five churches built within the walls of the medieval citadel, as well as the town hall and the residence of the parish priest.

He even remembered the names of the churches: Santa Maria del Monte, at the top of the castle; Santa Catarina, Santa Maria delle

Grazie, with three altars near where there must have been water wells; Santo Spirito, and Sant'Antonio.

Incredible! He remembered the yellowed pages of that book perfectly and, while noticing the squared stones that had lain for centuries on the disinhibited soil, he imagined how life could have slowly dispersed from this place, the cradle of its direct descendants. Balzo di Montegallo, the main town, the seat of the local institutions, rose up after 1500. And given that the word Balzo meant a cliff, it had really been a leap off the Mount.

They reached the top, the RAI relay tower; next to it, the large cross built by the family of Cardinal Taliani on the occasion of the Holy Year of 1950.

At the foot of the cross, a body with a slashed throat; all around, Carabinieri both in uniform and in street clothes. They weren't yet aware of the presence of the four.

"But that's one of the water engineers. It's the Roman. His name is Francesco." It was Anselmo who spoke.

"His name was..." Tony corrected him.

"Then there is a connection with the other murder."

"The water," said Maurizio confirming Giulia's observation.

"But if the only suspect is the victim, then who's the killer? What did you hear the two Carabinieri say? That he was the one they were looking for?" Giulia was in a hurry to put some semblance of order to what was becoming the story of the year. And it was she who had the advantage over all the other journalists. Nobody else knew that the only suspect was dead. Nobody even knew he had been the only suspect. Or the second victim. Had to be a victim. Impossible to commit suicide by slashing your own throat. She looked closer. The corpse's hands and feet were tied.

Rome
Caffè della Pace
Sunday, June 17, 20XX
7:23 PM

Simply water: pure, transparent, limpid, reliable. Water never betrayed you, water never surprised you. Commendatore Silvio Forlan didn't like surprises. He held between his fingers a trusted glass of water. He gazed at it against the backlighting, while the useless words of Senator Emidio Cecchini buzzed in his ears.

Seated across the table, the Senator had been reassuring him about the consequences of the murder in Montegallo.

Forlan had just received the news of Francesco Baldacci's death and of the involvement of his other employee, Ian Vladic. This had put him very much on edge. More than that, it had really pissed him off.

He had already counted on the profits from a business as simple as the water he was drinking. Instead, there were two dead people with the further complication of a complicit and terrified mayor and a hoard of journalists who had caught the whiff of a bloody scoop.

"You'll see, there won't be any problems. The mayor has only postponed it for a week. Monday June 25 you'll officially have the concession for the utilization of the water springs of Montegallo and starting on Tuesday June 26..."

"I'm going tomorrow."

"Where?"

"To clear up the whole damn mess."

He let the glass drop. Nobody came to clean up the broken shards on the paving stones. The bill had already been paid, and the only waiter had other things to think about.

The flow of passersby coming from the Piazza Navona was constant and dense, equal to that headed towards it.

The two got up and fell in line with the procession of tourists, strollers, flower sellers, of boys and girls for whom Monday was still a long way off.

"I think it would be better not to go. You'll end up attracting the attention not only of the press, but of the inhabitants. You'll put the mayor in a tough spot."

They were walking side by side but Forlan wasn't talking and maybe not even listening.

"Listen to me for once. Your presence won't help. Send someone if you want, but don't go yourself. Someone who can stay in the shadows. At least for now..."

Forlan still didn't say anything, while the Senator tried to insinuate himself into the silence which he had interpreted as a moment of uncertainty on the part of his companion. On the contrary, the king of mineral water had already decided on the next move.

They reached the big Roman piazza between the church of Sant'Agnese and Bernini's fountain. Staring into the void under the obelisk held up by the four rivers, a masterpiece of the sculptor's art, Forlan said, "I want the signed decision on Wednesday June 20."

"But..."

"No 'buts.' I'm going tomorrow to talk to Assergi. Good evening."

He walked off at a fast pace, leaving Senator Cecchini suspended in his own — more useless than ever — thoughts.

His eyes followed the haughty gait of the entrepreneur. The man never gave way and anyone who crossed his path he cut off without batting an eyelash, as if it was the most natural thing in the world. He commanded respect, or if not that, fear. "It must be the well-groomed mustache, that gaze that doesn't see anything or anybody, that decisive bearing, or the unbuttoned white shirt," Cecchini thought. So he straightened his spine, raised his eyes, and undid a couple of buttons.

He started to walk towards the Brazilian embassy. In thirty feet he had five collisions: one with a pair of Germans, one with a Nigerian vendor of sunglasses, with a pregnant woman, with a man holding a pitbull on a leash — luckily for him, muzzled — and with an aged Polish nun.

Depressed, he stopped. He got out his cellphone and called Lady T who answered right away.

"Hi, it's Emidio...yes, that's right, Forlan's friend. I want to make a date for tomorrow. At 10 PM, that would be great. Please, with all the necessary equipment. Goodbye 'til tomorrow."

Heartened by the perfume of transgression, he continued his walk, making his apologies.

Montegallo
The Mount
Sunday June 17, 20XX
7:29 PM

Marshal Moser had the feeling he was being watched. He turned around suddenly and saw a bush move behind him.

Marshal Fianchini and the other officers were busy surveying the area around Francesco Baldini's corpse.

Moser made the agreed upon signal to be quiet. He perked up his ears.

"... damn I'm thirsty."

"Be quiet or they'll find us"

"I've got a bottle of water in the car."

"What would I do with water?"

Moser crept up on them without making a sound.

He recognized the quartet awkwardly camouflaged in the vegetation.

"Come out, step up!"

The first to emerge was Tony. "Good evening, Marshal."

The last to appear, from behind a juniper bush, was Anselmo.

"All right, before I completely lose my patience, try to explain to me what you're doing here. Calmly please. And don't give me any run-around." There was an explosion of explanations. The incoherent choir irritated the officer even more.

Understanding the situation, Giulia Cantarini took him aside. "Marshal, as you already know, I'm a journalist and I'm trying to do my job. At the moment, I must say, with great results. Even with all the other journalists flocking around here, nobody knows what I know. The only suspect is dead. With all probability he was killed by the same person who killed the teacher. We're dealing with a collaborator of Forlan's and the only traceable link between the two crimes is the concession of the springs that the mayor is on the point of granting to the Roman entrepreneur. I know that you are groping in the dark seeing that the only suspect is dead."

"Signora..."

"Cantarini."

"Signora Cantarini, what are you getting at?"

"Nothing, just that this evening I'll be writing the article for my paper revealing the particulars of the investigation underway. But I suppose you won't like that very much."

"It certainly isn't convenient for us."

"Naturally. How about if I make you a proposition? I'll keep this confidential. I'll write a version that sticks to the information you provided at the press conference. You'll get at least twenty four hours more to keep the identity of the second victim secret, but in exchange you'll keep me informed about everything. I'll promise not to reveal anything until the murderer is caught, or anyway, until the investigation is closed, but at the same time I'll prepare a report of the entire business that I'll publish only when it's all over. Up until then I'll stick to the official version."

"Signora Cantarini, I can't possibly accept. I'm not authorized to provide information, even for the benefit of the inquiry."

"But you don't have to talk to me. Look, today I made friends with your wife, she's very nice. She invited me in for coffee, we chatted about this and that..."

"Leave my wife out of this."

"Don't worry and, above all, don't be mad at Gilda. She doesn't know I'm a journalist. I also made friends with your son. A wonderful boy."

"That's enough. I'm taking all of you back to town and you can thank heaven that I'm not arresting you."

"Marshal, think about it. Tonight I'll go and have a cup of coffee with your wife and if by chance, there is a folder on the table with copies of the two murder reports, and then she has to get something from the bedroom..."

"Signora Cantarini, goodbye. Accompany the gentlemen back to town and be assured..."

"We have a car, thank you," Giulia said with a wink.

Montegallo
Forest Ranger Station
Sunday June 17, 20XX
7:41 PM

Paolo Corbucci, Forest Service inspector, parked his official vehicle in the meadow next to the station where he had been working for twelve years. The parking lot, usually adequate to accommodate the visitors' cars, was full and the overflow had been forced to occupy this muddy field.

The work day wasn't over yet, and more things had happened in these hours than in the twelve years he had been assigned to the Montegallo station. He was worn out. Two corpses discovered in the briefest span of time, one after the other. Two murders had fallen right into their hands, who knows from where. He and his colleague Marco Martino had discovered the second body—the second one too, right after the first one. Francesco Balducci, the only suspect in the murder of Angeletti, had been found after hours of exhausting searches of woods and fields involving seven men. Totally flabbergasting. Adding insult to injury. Not only had the suspect been turned into a victim, which was a big disappointment, but the circumstances of the death—murder—had demanded the implementation of all required procedures

Since the two of them had found the body, they were the ones who had to secure the scene of the crime and provide details of the discovery to the Carabinieri. Given his special knowledge of the area, the officers had chosen Martino for the added duty of helping the troopers.

Paolo had gone back to the station for a routine meeting organized a week ago with the local hunters assigned to thin the population of wild boars. Periodically it was necessary to cull the herd within the park, so year after year a team of hunters was assembled in coordination with the forest rangers and put to work.

The subject of the meeting would have been what limits to apply, above all the numbers and the characteristics of the beasts to be killed per capita.

The sense of exhaustion and the band that was tightening around his head at the temples would stay with him for the duration of the meeting.

"Fucking shit..." Mud everywhere, splashed all over his camouflage. Getting out of his car he had put his boots into a quagmire, one of the many puddles that covered the dirt surface hidden from the sun by the thick shade of firs and cypress. The heavy spring rains had made things worse.

Where there wasn't water, there was mud, a thick and insidious layer. It wouldn't go away until summer... full summer.

It wasn't that bad, Paolo tried to console himself, the day after tomorrow his uniform was going to the laundry anyway. When he entered the meeting room in the station, more than twenty hunters were already complaining that he was five minutes late.

They were just about all residents of Montegallo, and all experts in the art of hunting, a centuries old tradition in this little center of the Apennines.

Gualtiero Marcucci, Serafino Petrucci, and Giorgio Zappa of Balzo. Antonio Marcucci and Luigi Toce of Pistrino. Marcello Tristani and Giuseppe Grossi of Forca. Sante Mancini of Propezzano. Gustavo Macchia and Giuseppe Piattelli of Uscerno. Mario Zappa of Castro. Guerrino Marini of Rigo. Antonio Mancini of Interprete. Nicola Fratini of Piano.

The inspector was assailed with dozens of questions that had nothing to do with the orders of the day. The preferred subject, obviously, was the murder of the teacher. And they still didn't know anything about Baldacci.

Paolo went straight to the point.

"Gentlemen, I can't tell you anything regarding the investigation, so let's deal with the matters that have to do with us for right now."

That took less than an hour. Basically everybody there, unlike other times, was eager to finish. They were in a hurry to dive back into the crime coverage, which for the first time in human memory put Montegallo at the center of national attention.

They were already winding down — with the ritual recommendations to be careful — when a special agent entered the room and handed him a folder.

He concluded the meeting quickly and set to reading the documents. They dealt with an update in the investigation. The Carabinieri had sent him the photos of the imprints of the boots collected by RIS at Santa Maria in Pantano, but the real news was that the same imprints had been found near the site of the second murder. This confirmed the disquieting hypothesis that there was one killer.

"Second murder? Shit! Think what the newspapers..."

The cast of the boot print clearly showed a sole with heavy use on the right corner of the heel; this created an unbalanced and unusual shape where the foot hit the ground.

Paolo Carbucci looked carefully at the photo of the cast, then turned to the short attached description. He didn't reach the bottom. The imprint! He turned to look at it. Incredible, he had the impression he had already seen it. But where? At Santa Maria in Pantano. No, he would have remembered that. In a situation like the one he had found himself in there, he would never have forgotten a detail of that type.

Nothing to be done. Maybe it was just his imagination.

Suddenly a lightning bolt of memory.

The mud!

The imprint was in the field outside the station, near the parked cars. He had seen it when, already muddied, he had walked around trying not to stumble into another puddle.

He ran outside. A number of hunters were already gone, but even more were still there gabbing, and some of these stood right on the dug up field.

He started to go back and forth over the meadow with his face down to scrutinize the ground but it was useless. The surface was trampled, the cars that had already left had driven over it and cancelled the footprint before leaving their own. No trace of the one he was looking for.

Raising his eyes, he saw that those present had stopped talking and were observing him with curiosity. Someone asked what he was doing. He didn't answer.

He could have made everybody go back inside and called the police, but he wasn't so sure anymore of what he had seen. An official action without any basis, he would really be held up to ridicule.

Marshal Moser was a friend, he could explain it to him. He got out his cellphone and gave him a call.

"Hi Marshal, it's Paolo. I have to talk to you."

"Go ahead."

"I received the documents you sent over and I think I've got a lead about the footprint."

"Okay. Can you meet me up at the Mount?"

"On the Mount, sure. I'll be right there."

His day wasn't over yet.

Montegallo
Village of Corbara
Morgana Bucci's House
Sunday June 17, 20XX
8:53 PM

"Augusto, shall we go?"

"I'm coming."

The Count had not been out of his room since Morgana had shown him to it.

The old stone house was recently renovated and furnished with all the modern comforts.

Augusto Piloni de Castris came down the wooden staircase that connected the bedrooms to the sizeable living room, a masculine version of Wanda Osiris, the classic Italian actress; the elegant gait, radiant smile and a trail of scent that floated on the air. Only the roses were lacking.

Morgana was waiting purse in hand at the bottom of the stairs. "Usually it's the women who make you wait."

"You're right, but I like the room very much. I enjoyed a nice shower and made some phone calls."

"Good, I'm glad. But we have to go now, we're late for a date with Giulia and two other friends you already know. The two guests of the mayor at your party."

"It's a small world."

"Oh right! Darn, I didn't think about that. If you want we can dine somewhere else but...in my opinion they're good guys."

"No, it's not a problem. Let's go."

"Good, they're expecting us at nine at the restaurant in the piazza in Balzo."

They got into the Count's Porsche Cayenne.

"By the way, how were you able to make calls? There isn't any cellphone signal in Corbara, and there isn't a land line in your room."

"Satellite telephone. There's one here too," he answered, indicating the set up between the two seats.

"You said you wanted to take a vacation."

"Yes, but sometimes I can't take my own advice."

Montegallo
Town Road — Santa Maria in Lapide
Sunday June 17, 20XX
9:00 PM

He had to take action again.

He had immediately consulted the Grand Master and, as always, he had been enlightened. The Master had shown him the path, and he had also indicated the most favorable place.

He felt a huge need to sleep, to close his eyes and sink into the dark, but he could not do that.

His legs were heavy. When possible he went on foot and in the last twenty four hours he had walked more than ever. He set out on an uphill path that took him directly from the forest ranger station to the hill above Balzo, cutting across the route of Paolo Corbucci who was stuck in the traffic that clogged the town.

The risk of being recognized was too high. The forest ranger had discovered something and had to be stopped.

The Grand Master had explained that the third place he had to make a human sacrifice was as essential as the other two. To go to the Mount — his objective — Corbucci would have to take the road that led to Santa Maria in Lapide, the other church in Montegallo more than a thousand years old, also dating back to 700 AD. A few kilometers before that, at the first turn, right at the elbow of the curve, was the entrance to the dirt road that went to the summit of the Mount.

He had listened to Corbucci's telephone call, and had seen him suddenly get nervous. He had heard him talking to the marshal about a footprint.

He hid himself behind a bush, taking a second to catch his breath. He had started running after the telephone call with the Grand Master. He thought he wouldn't make it in time, but now he saw the flash of the lights of the green Panda 4X4 coming from Balzo.

The car was about to turn into the dirt road that led to the place Moser had specified for the appointment.

He jumped into the middle of the road and started waving his arms, forcing the car to stop.

"What's going on? What are you doing here?"

"Inspector, there's been an accident. A car has gone off the road."

"Where?"

"Down there, at the curve by the dump."

"I can't deal with it right now. Call somebody else."

"No, no! I heard screaming. Maybe it's too late. Let's go!"

"Okay, get in."

He took his place on the seat next to the driver. With one hand he pretended to pull up his knee sock, while actually grasping of the handle of the knife hidden in his shoe.

"Where exactly?" Then like a bolt of lightening, Paolo Corbucci had a terrifying doubt. "Show me your shoes."

"What?"

"Show me your shoes. Take off your shoes, I said."

From the initial sense of panic to the reassuring serenity of presentiment. The idea of hiding the blade in his shoe had come at the last minute. A sign. The Grand Master and the cause he was fighting for were just.

He bent forward. He undid the knots of his laces. With his right hand he grasped the knife. He sat back up slowly and with the shoe in his left, he succeeded in concealing the weapon for the large part of the trajectory of straightening up.

When Paolo Corbucci became aware of the threat, it was too late. The blade was silhouetted in the shadows and struck forward towards the breast of the incredulous forest ranger.

It pierced his heart with the first blow.

Years of hunting and poaching wild boars, hares, deer. But also experience with farm animals, pigs, rabbits, sheep.

He knew how to use a knife. He knew where and how to strike. In the end, meat is just meat, blood just blood, and a heart is just a heart.

Paolo Corbucci died instantly.

Putting on a pair of latex gloves, he cleaned the door handle he had been forced to touch and then got out of the car. No one travelling on the main road could see him. He cleaned the outside handle too. Back inside the car, he pushed the body of the forest ranger out of the driver's seat, started the engine, and headed for Santa Maria in Lapide. There was nobody there. He forced the door open like he had at Santa Maria in Pantano, carried the dead body inside on his back, and left it in front of the altar.

Montegallo
Carabinieri Station
Marshal Moser's Residence
Sunday June 17, 20XX
10:34 PM

The living room of Signora Gilda Armili Moser seemed to come out of a tourist brochure from Cortina d'Ampezzo, the alpine ski resort. Order, good taste, and style — the perfect mountain chalet.

Right away Giulia Cantarini noticed the folder with the police insignia, placed on the wooden table next to a vase of flowers. In a flash she planned how she would put it in her purse as soon as Gilda could be distracted.

Massimo, the little boy, had already gone to bed when she showed up for coffee.

She had abandoned her four companions at the restaurant savoring biscotti and vino cotto.

Because of her petty blackmail she had expected a cool and distant welcome, but instead she found a smiling Gilda ready to exchange a little gossip between women. Almost as if she was released from her duty of being the marshal's wife.

Maybe Gilda was feeling stressed. Of course she had been under pressure ever since the beginning of all this business, forced to barricade herself in the house to escape the curious and the reporters. And her husband kept telling her to keep her lips sealed, even if it was highly improbable that she would have a word to say given Moser's rigidity. He was a man who never confided anything.

In any case, a day in hell for Gilda Armili Moser.

The two women talked for half an hour, more or less. About loving to garden, about life in a little town lost in the Apennines, and her, from Venice. But at the end of every phrase, she always added that she was happy with her choice and that she liked it here.

At a certain point she confessed she was fascinated with journalism. As a girl studying at the Mameli classics high school, that had always been her dream, her passion.

From journalism, to children, to the most convenient strategies for doing the shopping, Signora Gilda Armili Moser couldn't be distracted. She never left her seat.

Giulia tried to send her a subliminal message by standing up. "Excuse me Gilda, may I use the bathroom?"

"Come on, I'll take you there."

While they were commenting on the hydromassage bath the marshal was so proud of, Moser himself burst into the house. Speak of the Devil!

"Gilda, Gildaaaa! I need a clean uniform. I need to take a fast shower and go right back out."

"It's in the closet. But why all this hurry? Why do you have to leave again?"

"Come one. Get it for me. Hurry! I have to get going. They found Paolo Corbucci. Dead. Probably the same killer, who's obsessed with churches. They found his body at Santa Maria in Lapide, left on the altar."

He came into the bathroom with only a towel wrapped around his waist.

"Cecco, we have a guest."

"Hi Marshal. Well, you keep yourself fit don't you? In pretty good shape I'd say."

"Cantarini, you're pestering me."

"By the way, is it definite that it's the same killer? And who is Paolo Corbucci?"

"An inspector in the Forest Service and a friend of Cecco's. Poor fellow!"

"I've told you a thousand times not to call me Cecco in front of outsiders. But yes, it's true. Paolo was a good friend. He telephoned me because he thought he had a good idea about the identity of the killer, and I told him to join me on the Mount. But he never arrived."

"So he was killed for that?"

"Listen Cantarini, this is confidential information."

"You remember, we made a pact and I'm a reliable person."

"Okay, I want to trust you. In fact I have to. I want to find that bastard and if tomorrow you publish the details that you've discovered it could put the entire investigation in danger. Plus my son told me that you have the same color eyes as the fairy in his favorite fairytale."

"What a boy! Who did he get that from?"

"I know where he got it from. When he was young Cecco was always surrounded by girls."

"And quit it with Cecco!"

"Come on, by now Giulia is like one of the family."

"Oh, one of the family? Well then it's a plot! Listen Gilda. This is serious business. Very serious. I have things to do, so let me take this blessed shower. Out, please."

"Marshal, how do you plan to proceed? What idea did Paolo Corbucci have? Who is the killer?"

"I don't know! If I knew I wouldn't be here. I've called together all the licensed hunters who attended a routine meeting with Paolo at the station. He must've gotten suspicious there, after he received the photos of the footprint of the murderer."

"A footprint?"

"Exactly. An imprint taken from the dusty pavement at Santa Maria in Pantano. Now excuse me, I'm in a hurry. Can I get on with my shower?"

He pushed the two women towards the door. Giulia put up a final resistence. "One last thing, are all the churches up here named for the Madonna?"

"What are you getting at?'

"Nothing. Just curious."

"Can I wash up now?"

"Excuse me, I was first in line." Giulia shut herself in the bathroom.

Montegallo
Village of Corbara
Morgana Bucci's House
11:41 PM

Dinner had been eaten in the hope, shared by all, that it would be over with as soon as possible. For Morgana the tension at the table was unbearable. Maurizio's taciturn distance was palpable as was Tony's unconcealed hostility.

The Count had comported himself as a true gentleman, forcing himself to stay calm. But he had not succeeded in completely hiding all the anger that the offense committed by the two Romans continued to foment within him.

Giulia put the icing on the cake by abandoning them for a work appointment.

Tired of the situation, Morgana grasped any plausible excuse to end the evening early and asked Augusto to take her home.

On the way, neither of them acknowledged the tense atmosphere. Once they were home they found themselves talking about books. While the Count closely examined the volumes lined up on the impressive walnut shelf system that took up an entire wall of the living room, Morgana arranged the wood in the fireplace. The family coat of arms was sculpted above the mantel. She had decided to light a fire, but not because it was cold.

"Morgana, you really have quite a library here."

"Thank you. I'm very proud of these volumes. Some of them are very old."

"I see, I see. I too am very interested in esotericism, but here you have some truly unique examples."

The fire flared up around two oak logs and one of beech, the flames rose higher. Morgana turned off the chandelier and lit three candles in three different parts of the room. "You see that one with the red leather cover? That is..."

"... 'The Heptameron' by Pietro de Abano, 1535, in Latin." Augusto finished her sentence, letting his finger slide down the volume so extraordinary as to capture all of his attention.

Morgana brought out a bottle of red wine, a house present from the Count's personal reserve.

"This one is the 'Liber Incantatium Exorcismorum et Fascinationum Variarum,' dating back to the 15th century, one of the rare copies is conserved in Munich. This one, on the other hand, is the 'De Nigramancia' by Bacon, also in Latin."

Lit by the candles, and the flames of the fireplace, she found herself admiring his face, as he transformed and intensified.

Augusto Piloni de Castris caressed the books with a fixed gaze as if in a trance, his fingers tapered like tentacles ready to envelop and clutch.

She sat down on the sofa curious to see where her guest was going to end up.

"Of course, but of course..." the Count continued, consumed by the fascination of the ancient documents, "This is the perfect place to conserve such treasures. Since the dawn of time, this land has been the cradle of occult forces, hidden from the eyes of the simple and skeptical, depository of arcane energy of the spirits and of nature. In the bowels of the Sibillini Mountains pulse the veins of the spiritual body of the human dimension, a dimension that evolves and rises only with the help of the sacred celestial presence. This lies dormant, hidden in nature in the four elements; in the living fabric of these mountains one of these elements runs powerful and pure. Water. The streams, arteries; the springs, beating hearts; and the Lago di Pilato, highest altar of the spirits only accessible by means of the pure water of the divine mountains, mountains that have hosted for millennia the secret forces of the beyond. And woe be to the men who not only have ignored these forces for centuries, but are now trying to extract ignoble profits by exploiting the blood of the earth, the blood of the Sibillini."

Morgana listened, petrified by the mystic delirium of the Count. His voice suddenly had a familiar sound. Certainly she was not surprised by what the Count was saying. She well knew that for more than a thousand years, the Lago di Pilato had been the goal of necromancers, sorcerers, and devotees of esoteric and demonic rituals. She knew well that Mt. Vettore and Mt. Sibilla were sites endowed with mystical auras of particular importance in the geog-

raphy of the occult world. What confused her more than anything
was the deranged face of Augusto; lit up, in the dimness, by the
tongues of fire that flickered in the fireplace and from the dancing
sisters on wax pedestals, it was distorted into a grotesque grimace.
The deep black eyes sparkled, possessed by a morbid light. That
gaze reminded her of something. But she didn't have the courage to
say what that was.

After a brief pause, the Count continued to talk with the same
rapture. "Since the beginning, hope has been feminine. The creative force is feminine. Fertility, which is the same as salvation,
is feminine. This is shown in heaven as on earth. The cult of the
Queen Mother, recognized and renewed from the beginnings of
Christianity through the deification of the Madonna. And it is exactly in these places that the priests established, on earth, the celestial map of the symbol of heaven, the constellation of the Virgin
Mary, a foundation that is planted in the bowels of this sacred land.
Often, next to them pours forth springs of water, pure and purify-
ing. Their spiritual force lights the fire of the initiates and the wind
that breathes through the illuminated minds of the elect lifts the
spirits in a vertiginous ascent towards the culmination of that voyage which is life."

"I know this theory." Morgana remembered having read something of this sort and tried to awaken Augusto from the alarming
monologue. She didn't like the ecstatic tone and the raving turn
that the soliloquy had taken. "I have here a rather recent book by a
scholar from Ascoli. The title is actually 'The Constellation of the
Virgin,' and it maintains that between Montegallo, Montemonaco,
and the west slope of Mt. Vettore there are nine churches named
after the Madonna that, seen from above, represent perfectly the
stars that make up Virgo. It should be here..." She went towards
the lowest shelf of the bookcase. "Here it is. Look..."

The Count wasn't paying attention, the grimace on his face
ever more contorted, his gaze far off, his lips distorted in a peculiar
sneer.

There was silence. Augusto slowly approached the glasses
which his hostess had prepared. Three steps, and his features became human again.

His lips touched his goblet. He tipped it towards his face without breaking eye contact with Morgana. For a moment she brightened up and sipped, thinking to share a toast with her guest.

Augusto did not drink.

Even her feminine intuition could not read his opaque expression.

Montegallo
Village of Astorara
Maurizio Verdimani's House
Sunday June 17, 20XX
11:50 PM

The last drop of vodka had already been drained from the bottle.

Ending up like the rest in the glass clutched by Tony, who continued to stare with disappointment at the empty upside down container. If he could have, he would have wrung it out.

"Crap, it's empty! Mauri, do you have another one? Mauri? Mauriziooo!!"

Maurizio floated in a state of lucid dread. The unbearable doubt that his personal paradise—this house, that patch of sky that he was looking at dazed through the bedroom window, those little cracks that indicated the beams suspended over his head—might not actually be his.

The serious possibility of losing it to Ecosystem, about which he knew absolutely nothing, tormented him. So...perhaps he could utilize these days of forced presence in Montegallo to resolve the question.

Unfortunately he couldn't glimpse any solution. The purchase had seemed above board to him, but the lawyer from Ecosystem surely must have an ace up his sleeve. Why then were they prepared to pay double? If they had legal title to the claim, their legitimate property, why double the price? The only answer had to be the time factor. Ecosystem was in a hurry. Why?

"Mauriziooo! Mauriziooo!"

"What's up?"

Tony was yelling from the kitchen. Slumped in a chair, he was talking to himself about the beauty of Giulia Cantarini... about his disappointment at being abandoned in the middle of dinner... about the tragedy of existence—above all, of *his* existence, destined for misunderstanding and miscommunication—and, a thing even more serious, about the tragedy of the condition of a thirsty vodka drinker forced into abstinence by a cynical and cheating destiny that had caused this running out of stock.

"Tony, enough! You're stinking drunk."

"Of course I'm drunk, but not stinking drunk... a little drunk. If you were to get me more vodka, I could give you the satisfaction of being right. Even if it isn't vodka, it would be the same. How about some whiskey?"

"I don't have any more alcohol. You've finished it all off."

"You're right, excuse me. We're friends, right? Eh? We're friends, you and me, right Mauri?" He stood up trying to keep his balance and then draped himself around Maurizio's neck in a ridiculous attempt to give him a big hug.

"Yes, yes, we're friends. But be good. Sit back down."

"Then give me a kiss, my friend."

"What are you doing? Cut it out! You reek of alcohol. That's enough!" With a push he made him sit down again.

"There you see? You always treat me bad, even when I need help."

"Sorry, I didn't mean to. It's just that my head is full of doubts. I've got a problem that torments me day and..."

"Mauri, I can't face it anymore. I live a life I don't understand anymore, don't control anymore. I seem to have lost the meaning of everything."

"Listen Tony, I'm at risk of losing my house."

"Your house! Your house! You're talking to me about a house. I'm talking to you about an inner anguish, about a malaise of life. About the fact that I'm in despair. And you talk to me about a house... I don't give a flying fuck about this god-forsaken place... of uncontaminated nature... of the authenticity of these asshole mountaineers. I want to breathe smog! I want a stinking city made of asphalt and cement! I want shitheads who jerk me around smiling in my face and stabbing me in the back! I want the pollution of the soul. I am polluted!"

"No, you're a shithead egotist, and drunk to boot."

"Huh, me? Go f..."

At this moment a roar erupted outside. It got progressively louder, reached its climax and then little by little went away. Maurizio and Tony pressed their noses to the window.

A huge black truck, like the one that almost ran over Tony as soon as he arrived in Montegallo, had left the main road and was climbing the dirt track not far from Maurizio's house. It was headed towards the zone right under the massive rock face of Mt. Vettore, a zone recently struck by a big mudslide, a zone famous for an important water spring. One of the many in Montegallo, one of the springs that Acque Sane was seeking concessions for, one of those at the center of the killer's attention, and therefore, of everybody's attention. Maurizio remembered the fresh water of this spring, water that he had gone to get with his father who had suffered from high blood pressure, water that his father had always claimed worked miracles.

Tony left his friend to observe the dark of a once again quiet night. Silence can be pitiless if you are prey to those dark thoughts that assail men in certain stages of life.

It was just too much. He collapsed into a chair, in front of an empty bottle, with his hands in his hair, overwhelmed by a volcano of frustration, regret, and unresolved expectations. All wrapped up in a fog of alcohol more or less evaporated by the stress of the discussion and the sudden noise of the black truck.

Maurizio continued to stare into the dark in search of a star that would indicate the right way.

After a while, as if struck by lightning, Tony raised his head, and said in a firm voice, "I need to take action. Maurizio, come with me now. I have to do something, and you have to keep me company. But on the way tell me everything regarding this house business. Tell me what the problem is and we'll tackle it together."

"What? Quit it, you're in a pitiful state."

"Listen, I have to go. If you think I'm not capable, then you have to come too, otherwise I'm going by myself."

"Go where you want! And don't bust my balls."

"Okay, all right, bye."

He stood up, unsteady on his legs, and took a few steps. Near the door he stumbled and fell. He struggled to his feet. Without looking at his friend, he left.

After a couple of seconds he returned.

Maurizio shook his head, as if to say, "I knew it."

He watched Tony go into his room and come back out right away, blathering, "The keys, I forgot the car keys." Seeing him stumble at the same place as before and get to his feet with the same obstinacy as before, he decided to follow him. "Wait! I'll go with you. Wait! I'll drive."

Montegallo
Forest Ranger Station
Sunday June 17, 20XX
11:55 PM

Giulia Cantarini was clinging to the second floor windowsill of the Montegallo Forest Ranger Station. Inside Marshal Moser was meeting with the hunters licensed to cull the wild boar, in an emergency session called after finding the corpse of Paolo Corbucci.

The atmosphere was heavy with anxiety. Those present had guessed the seriousness of the situation from the lateness of the hour and the professional and distant demeanor of the troopers, starting with Moser.

Giulia had waited until they were all inside, then she had shinned up with the help of a downspout.

Because there were so many people in the room, the window had been opened a crack.

The voice of the marshal reached her clearly. He took the roll call. Everybody was there, except one. Giuseppe Grossi.

The confusion of the investigators became tangible. The meeting was immediately cut short. All of the hunters were told to remain at their disposition. An order was issued to search for Giuseppe Grossi.

She heard Marshal Moser plainly. "Make a thorough investigation of Giuseppe Grossi. I want to know every last detail, work, relationships, friends; past, present, and future. Do you understand? So why the hell are you still here? Get going!"

Giulia took it all in, but the fact that Grossi was the only one not to show up did not necessarily make him the killer. Certainly it indicated a concrete direction for investigation.

Now that the meeting was over, the acrobatic reporter decided to descend from her perch. Halfway down she set her foot wrong and fell onto one of the parts of her anatomy generally most admired. In this instance it displayed itself as highly useful in the protection of the rest. The meager height contributed not a little to the positive outcome of the fall, but the thud attracted the attention of someone.

Francesco Moser looked out the window. The picture presented to him was that of a smiling Giulia Cantarini, still sitting on the ground. "Hi Marshal, how's it going?"

"Don't move. I'm coming down right away."

A Road in Montegallo
Tony's Alfa Spider
Monday June 18, 20XX
12:15 AM

"Slow down! Shit!"

Tony had insisted on driving.

"Okay, all right, all right. Calm down and go on explaining to me about your house."

"But where are we going?"

"Don't you worry about that, finish telling me that story of . . . what's the name of the company that wants to buy you out?"

"Ecosystem . . . and watch the road!"

The actor took the curve a little too wide. "In my opinion there's something going on. First of all you have to find out what the irregularity in your purchase was — if there was one — and then verify who is the real owner. That is, you have to do something. You can't just stand still, locked in your own thoughts, in the hope that a miracle will fix everything. And then, excuse me, if this Ecosystem has already bought it, why would they pay for it twice?"

"You can tell that they're in a hurry."

"Exactly. Why are they in a hurry? There's something behind this. And who are they? What kind of business are they in? Who is it exactly, who's in such a rush?"

"I don't know. I don't know anything. And don't look at me, look at the road!"

"I'm trying to tell you that you've got to inform yourself. You have to know who you're dealing with and what they're doing."

"Brake! Braaake!"

The tires screeched to a stop on the asphalt. Beyond the windshield, lit up by the headlights, filed a pack of wild boars with the little ones following behind. After a few seconds of astonishment, Tony, without starting the car again, turned towards Maurizio, "You know who might be able to help you?"

"Who?"

"Giulia Cantarini, plus a local lawyer."

"A lawyer is obvious, but what does Giulia have to do with this?"

"What do you mean? She's a reporter, great at gathering information, so she's perfect for finding out what's behind all this."

"But come on, why would she do that?"

"Because it might be useful for an article, and then because in exchange we could tell her the facts about the other night, the accident with the killer."

"But what killer? You remember that the suspect is dead, murdered as well."

"That doesn't mean anything. She will definitely be interested, plus I have to find her anyway."

He took off peeling rubber, breaking the silence already interrupted too many times on this strange night in Montegallo.

"So it's her we're going after. And to do what?"

"I don't know, but I have to talk to her. If only I knew where she is."

"She's a guest at Morgana's house in Corbara."

"And how do you know that?"

"She said so earlier at dinner."

"Oh, I didn't hear that. And where is Corbara?"

"Go on, follow this road. I'll tell you where to turn. But I don't understand what you want to do. And go slow, asshole!"

Montegallo
Village of Corbara
Morgana Bucci's House
Monday June 18, 20XX
12:38 PM

During dinner Morgana had given her the house keys, so Giulia was not very worried when she arrived at the parking lot below her friend's village and saw that the Count's car wasn't there.

She smiled. Morgana and the fascinating Augusto had gone off together like two teenagers...

But now she had other things to think about.

She had to get started on a major piece for her paper, a piece that would go into the Tuesday edition. However, to draft the definitive version she would have to wait for the latest news on the search for Grossi. She had succeeded in convincing Moser to inform her immediately as soon as they found him. For today's edition she had stuck to the official version available to all the other journalists. But if they arrested the murderer during the night...if this Giuseppe Grossi was revealed as the killer of the Sibillini...she would be ready and above all, she would be the only one to have in hand all the particulars of the events. Following that, she would write her book, but the fact of being ahead of all the others right from the start would legitimize her as the top journalistic authority on what had happened.

In case Grossi's trail turned out to be a dead end, she wouldn't have submitted the article and could continue to accumulate materials and details in expectation of the most propitious moment.

Absorbed in this appraisal, she climbed up through the village byways. Corbara was built entirely into the rock, underneath a cliff on the summit of which, hidden in the vegetation, the hermitage of San Francesco kept watch.

When she entered the house she saw that the fire was lit. There were also some candles burning. On the table next to a bottle of Rosso Piceno Superiore — Piloni de Castris obviously — were two glasses, one half full and the other with a finger of wine at the bottom.

Setting her purse on the table, she read "Dear Giulia," on the piece of paper that she found there, "I leave the house at your disposal. Augusto and I are going to take a trip for a few days. See you soon, Morgana."

She thought about this for a few seconds, surprised. Enterprising, those two little lovebirds, for not being such spring chickens.

She turned on her laptop and set to work.

Organizing her notes, she added a few things and wrote down some considerations that she hadn't thought of until this moment. Then she stood up and started to pace around the room. She put some more wood on the fire. It was at that point that she looked around and had an unsettling sensation. Something wasn't right. She took up the piece of paper again. It had been written on the computer and printed out. Strange that Morgana would have left the house with the candles and fire still lit. She continued to look around seeking out a detail that would explain why she had this sensation. She took up her cellphone to call Morgana, but there was no signal. She decided to blow out the candles and turn on the lights. The room seemed, all of a sudden, sinister. The creative euphoria with which she had returned had been replaced by an inner discomfort, fruit of a sudden worry.

She was jolted by two blows on the front door. She screamed and then regained control in a hurry and went up close to the door. "Morgana, is that you?"

"Giulia, it's me, Tony. Maurizio's here too."

She opened the door. "What are you doing here?"

"No, it's just that...I have to tell you something and...also Maurizio wants to ask you a favor...so..."

"Come in. I'm working on the piece for tomorrow."

The two greeted her, excusing themselves as they came in. Maurizio was clearly embarrassed. Tony tried to act casual. To set the tone, he started by showing his appreciation of the beauty of the house, the taste with which it had been furnished, the pleasurable atmosphere that one breathed in.

"Where's Morgana?" he asked suddenly.

"She's not here. She left me a note saying she'd gone away with the Count for a few days. But it's strange."

Finally Maurizio opened his mouth. He was seated in a corner, holding a book which he had found lying on the arm of the couch. "What do you mean?"

"I don't know. It's just that it's not like Morgana to take off so impulsively."

Tony seized the moment. After taking a breath, he made the most absurd speech of his outlandish life. "But she did the right thing! I understand her very well. There are some things you do by instinct. In fact I'm here, at this hour, to tell you that . . . that . . . I'm in love with you and that . . . oh also that Maurizio wants to ask you a favor . . . about his house. Isn't that true, Maurizio? Look, you need to know that there's a business called Ecosystem that's trying to take away his house in Montegallo, and since you're a journalist and you're from around here, I got the idea that you could help him gather information about this Ecosystem . . . there has to be something going on. At least it should interest you. You might get a scoop."

Maurizio, with a burst of energy, interrupted this rant, "Tony, this is not the right time. Giulia has things to do and also, if I understand correctly, she's worried about Morgana. Come on, let's go."

"You're right. Yes, of course, excuse me. But still, maybe we can help. Giulia, what can we do? Do you want us to go look for her?"

Giulia, incredulous, lit a cigarette. It took her a bit to regain her composure.

"Listen Tony," she finally said, "I think you've had too much to drink. If you want, we'll talk again tomorrow."

"But what the fuck! I haven't drunk too much! In fact, I haven't drunk enough!" He exited, slamming the door.

Giulia and Maurizio looked at each other. Maurizio opened his arms wide, shrugging his shoulders. Giulia went outside. Maurizio stayed on the threshold. Tony got in the car, Giulia joined him, and they started to talk. So as not to intrude, Maurizio went back inside. He seated himself on the couch. The book was still there. At first he just leafed through it, then he started to read.

"The Constellation of the Virgin."

Montemonaco
Village of Tofe
The Church of Santa Maria in Casalicchio
Monday June 18, 20XX
12:40 AM

Giuseppe Grossi would not be working his usual night shift. He had taken the usual road to go as usual to the appliance factory. There he would have done his usual job on the assembly line.

But not that night.

About half way there he turned to the left, towards Montemonaco, and stopped in front of the church of Santa Maria in Casalicchio. Isolated, austere, silent. Comforting.

He got out of the car and looked up. Stars everywhere. The bell tower vied with the trees to reach them.

A breath of wind caused a pleasurable dizziness.

He had an appointment.

He went in. The door was open. The two naves were immersed in darkness, but he remembered the grand stone columns standing in the center.

"Come forward, brother." From the depths came a voice that he knew well.

"Master!"

With a torch in his hand, wrapped in a dark cloak and hidden under a pointed hood, the Master appeared out of nothingness. The Supreme Guide. His only reference point. He who had saved him from the confusion and the agony of an evil world.

"Come forward, come nearer."

Giuseppe took a few steps. He felt lighter. Around him and above him, the frescoes depicted episodes in the life of Christ. They flashed in the dark like dreamy seas in which he felt he was floating too, drifting along through an extraordinary day.

The Master took him by the arm and led him in front of the statue of St. Sebastian. The body pierced by the arrows of martyrdom attracted his attention. He stared at the wounds inflicted by the infidels' darts, from which spurted the saint's blood. In the trembling light of the torch, it seemed to glide down to fall on the pavement.

If he had seen it at another time — preferably in the light of day — he might have thought it looked amateurish.

Poor St. Sebastian.

The Master's hand grasped his face and forced him to turn until their eyes met.

"Congratulations, brother. You have done well. You have brought your task to its completion. You have defended the sacred springs. You have stopped the terrible threat."

"But Master, aren't you angry? I had to kill two extra people."

"It was necessary, and one final sacrifice is still needed to complete your work, so that your success will not be jeopardized. And by doing this you can attain the essence of the spirit."

"I'm listening, Master. What do I have to do? Who do I have to kill?"

"Yourself."

"What?"

"The ultimate sacrifice. The most important."

"But..."

"Come with me, follow me."

He allowed himself to be led. They came to a low window next to the entrance where he was forced to kneel and look outside.

"Do you see the mountain?"

"The Sibilla, Master."

"Exactly. From this window our predecessors observed the descent into the valley of the feminine spirits. In their presence the brothers swore their oath before the Queen Mother."

The light of the moon outlined the silhouette of Monte Sibilla.

"Have you brought the knife with you?"

"Yes Master. Here it is."

"Good. Now, with this sacred blade, slit the veins of your wrists. I myself will guide your hand. Trust me, brother. See, like this..."

The Master grasped Giuseppe's fist, which in its turn gripped the knife soaked with the blood of two men and one woman. He guided the trembling hand towards the crease of the left forearm and then, changing the grip, towards that of the right forearm.

Wounds inflicted longitudinally, inexorably.

Giuseppe clenched his teeth without letting out a cry. One tear glittered on his cheek. The Master caught a reflection of the moon on the face of the chosen one. With a paternal gesture, he caressed him, wiping away the one sign of weakness. Or perhaps, the last flash of reason.

He remained there in silence. The hooded mentor who held in an embrace of death the pupil with bloodied hands, an offering to a silent and innocent Sibilla.

After some hours, shortly before breathing his last breath, Giuseppe was able to say, "Master... Master..."

"Tell me brother, tell me!"

"... I know I fucked up."

And he expired.

- -

Montegallo
Village of Corbara
Morgana Bucci's House
Monday June 18, 20XX
3:07 AM

Two and a half hours had passed. Maurizio had fallen asleep on the couch in front of the fire, which by now was almost out.

He awoke with a start when the door slammed open. Giulia and Tony entered joking with each other.

"Were you sleeping?"

He stood up, stretched, look at his watch. "And a good thing too, otherwise I would have read the whole library. It's after three. I see that you two have been having a good time."

Giulia immediately changed the subject. "Tony has told me everything about your problem with Ecosystem. In my opinion, you need a lawyer, but I'll try to get you some information anyway. Who knows, we might find out something interesting. First of all, we need to know what this company's business is and why they want to buy your house at any price."

"But you two, are you engaged?"

"What do you mean engaged? At this stage of my life, I'm not really thinking about men. All my love is for my daughter, so..."

"Why are you even answering him?"

Someone knocked on the door. Giulia hurried to open it. "Maybe it's Morgana."

She was disappointed. Marshal Moser, without so much as a greeting, explained the reason for his visit. "We found him. I tried to call you but your cell phone wasn't picking up. So I came in person. With this, our pact is concluded."

"So he's the killer? Have you arrested him?"

"Yes we think he's the one, but we haven't arrested him. He's dead. He committed suicide while on his way to his job on the night shift."

Giulia was taking notes, "Where did you find him?"

"In the church of Santa Maria in Casalicchio, in one of the villages of Montemonaco."

"He was obsessed with churches. How did he kill himself?"

"He slit his veins with the same knife he used to kill the other three."

"What did you say was the name of the church?" The masculine voice caught the marshal by surprise. He had remained in the doorway, but when he heard Maurizio's question, he immediately took two steps inside.

"Signora Cantarini, I had expected more fairness on your part. Why didn't you tell me you weren't alone? Anyway, I have to go now, I've already spent too much time on you. I give you my regards and remind you again that the pact between us is over. The case is closed. Gentlemen, you can leave whenever you want to. Personally, I hope that will be soon."

Maurizio went up to him, "Wait, could you repeat for me what church he was found in?"

Moser turned to leave, but decided against it. He wasn't dealing with confidential news anymore. By the next day it would be in all the papers, so it was pointless to be rude.

"Santa Maria in Casalicchio."

"The other victims, where were they found?"

Impatient but calm, the marshal persevered in his attempt to be courteous. "The first was in the church of Santa Maria in Pantano, the second up on the Monte, the third in the church of Santa Maria in Lapide."

Satisfied with the answer, Maurizio picked up the book which he had just finished reading and held it out. "Read this, Marshal. The four places you just mentioned represent four stars in the constellation of the Virgin."

Tony and Giulia studied him, perplexed. They thought that maybe Maurizio was still befuddled, half asleep.

"What are you talking about?"

"According to the author of this book, there are nine churches distributed throughout this region that—seen from above—correspond to the projection in the sky of the constellation Virgo, visible to the bare eye from the Sibillini Mountains. Each of them is named after the Virgin Mary. Some of these don't exist anymore, like the church that was up on the Monte until the 1500's. The others that you listed are all part of this group."

"Signor Verdimani, right now I have other things to think about. We've found the killer, even though he's dead, and that's what matters. Your conjectures aren't very important anymore. The case is closed."

Moser got back in his car and left the three to reflect on the thesis of the stellar map recreated on earth by churches. A useless thesis, according to him.

The reporter seemed quite interested in Maurizio's observations. She could see a very catchy concept for the whole story: the killer of the Sibillini had followed a most precise scheme in the distribution of the bodies, including his own. She immediately started to flip though the book.

Her attention was drawn to the two pages that showed a map of the zone with the locations of the sacred buildings, and a drawing of the vault of heaven with the stars that make up Virgo. In effect, the lines traced from one star to the next formed a figure very similar to the one generated by connecting the points on the map.

While Giulia went on reading, Maurizio resumed his discourse. "As you can see, the zone is very extensive, it stretches as far as the Umbrian side of Mt. Vettore. Some of the marked churches have been destroyed, but their existence in the past is documented. In any case, I believe it's important to explore not so much the validity of the theory, but rather, what did the killer think of it? Was he aware of this connection and did it really mean something to him? By the way, you know who he is, right?"

The target of the question lifted her gaze from the book. "Yes, Giuseppe Grossi."

Tony spoke up for the first time. "Isn't he the cousin of your woodcutter friend?" he asked Maurizio.

"Yeah, that's him. But he doesn't seem like the type who reads books or is interested in these things. So maybe it's just a coincidence."

"Coincidence or not, I'm interested. But first, I have to get the story ready for the newspaper. Guys, I have work to do. You'll have to leave now, please."

"Good night, Giulia, and we're sorry we disturbed you." Maurizio started to go but Tony, instead of following him, wanted to know one last thing. He stared at the journalist.

"Would it bother you if I asked you a question?"

"Go right ahead."

"You don't happen to have a bottle of vodka, do you?"

THIRD PART

IL MESSAGGERO MARCHE

SIBILLINI SERIAL KILLER DEAD BY SUICIDE

The mystery of the Sibillini has been solved.

The corpse of Giuseppe Grossi, a twenty-nine year old factory worker from Montegallo, has been discovered. He is accused of the three crimes committed in the span of twenty-four hours on Sunday June 6 in Montegallo.

On Monday night, the perpetrator of the three murders was found dead inside the church of Santa Maria in Casalicchio, located in the village of Tofe in the township of Montemonaco. According to the investigators, the young man, aware that he was being hunted, panicked. In the grips of a serious mental disorder he ended his life by cutting his veins in an apparent ritual of repentance and redemption.

According to the reconstruction provided by the Carabinieri, various motives could have led to the commission of his crimes.

Digging into the past of his first victim, the preschool teacher Michela Angeletti, a troubling report has been discovered of an accusation of abuse involving Grossi's younger sister. The investigation that followed showed the complaint to be groundless, but during the fourteen years that have passed, Giuseppe evidently held a deep grudge. This grudge found a pretext for exploding in the controversy regarding the concession of territorial water rights by the mayor of Montegallo, Fabiano Assergi, to a private company. The relationship between the mayor and the teacher was apparently generally known, perhaps causing an unbalanced equation to take root in the brain of Giuseppe Grossi, who—according to local opinion—nurtured an obsession for the local aquatic resources. The investigators are inclined to believe that, more than a preoccupation with water, the crime reflects a pathological fixation on the actions of the mayor and his lover.

Michela Angeletti was kidnapped between Saturday night and Sunday morning, in circumstances still to be clarified. She was killed, without a doubt, in the church of Santa Maria in Pantano. Francesco Baldacci's murder was probably not planned in advance by the killer, but was committed to eliminate a casual witness.

The third crime, the execution of the forest ranger Paolo Corbucci, can be explained by the fact that the victim was about to unmask the guilty party. Corbucci had shared his suspicions with the Marshal Francesco Moser of the Carabinieri, who reported that these suspicions proved fundamental in the identification of the suspect.

A mystery remains regarding the places where Giuseppe Grossi left the corpses.

The most likely hypothesis concerning the killer's motives holds that he wanted to degrade his homeland's worth by defiling symbolic sites like Santa Maria in Pantano, Santa Maria in Lapide, and the Mount (site of the original settlement of Balzo). On the other hand the location of his suicide, Santa Maria in Casalicchio, could have been—still according to the investigators—purely fortuitous, as it was on the road that Grossi always took to work.

There are those who maintain, however, that the choice of these sacred places was not due to pure chance nor to a so-called "mystical" delirium, but to a well thought out plan by Grossi. Based on the theory of Dr. Renzo Roiati, a scholar from Ascoli, the locations where the corpses were found are the sites of churches named for the Madonna built in antiquity with the aim of reproducing on Earth the star map of the constellation of the Virgin. Some of these no longer exist today. This hypothesis takes into account the place where Francesco Baldacci's body was found, carried there after his death. Up until the 1500's, the original settlement of Balzo on the heights of the Mount also contained a church named for the Virgin Mary, which is included in the above mentioned map.

Is the case of the monster of Montegallo closed?

The investigators say yes.

In our view, however, something is still unclear. Above all, there are many unanswered questions.

Where does this tragic event leave the little Apennine villages of Le Marche?

Will the mayor persist in his project of privatizing the water concessions?

How will the inhabitants of Montegallo return to daily life?

An ugly story in a beautiful place.

Giulia Cantarini

Montegallo
Village of Balzo
Mayor's Office
Tuesday June 19, 20XX
11:22 AM

In front of Fabiano Assergi's desk sat Silvio Forlan and his companion, Simona Coda.

Spread on the table were the front pages of the daily newspapers.

Forlan seized a copy and threw it down under the eyes of the highly embarrassed Assergi.

"Now there are no more excuses. When do you think you'll respect our agreements?"

"Dr. Forlan, there's no need to take that attitude . . . I think that . . . within the week, I'll be able to get the concession approved."

"Very good. I'm staying here until then."

Without saying goodbye, the king of mineral water and his queen got up and left.

Fabiano Assergi, left alone, went back to reading Giulia Cantarini's article.

It was the one Forlan had thrown in his face.

He held onto the page for a few seconds and then picked up the phone and dialed a number.

"Hello, it's me. Silvio Forlan just left my office. Yeah, he's here along with his companion. What do you think about that?"

Montegallo
Village of Astorara
Maurizio Verdimani's House
Tuesday June 19, 20XX
11:44 AM

The shower beat down on Maurizio's body.

His spirit, also naked, tried to wash away the sense of impotence that filled him. He stood immobile, with the jet of hot water hammering the back of his neck.

He thought about all the sacrifices he'd made to buy this house.

He thought about how much his parents had wanted a place of their own in Montegallo, about how much he himself wanted it.

This had never been just a house, it was his personal ambition.

An ambition that he had been able to realize. Or, at least, he'd thought so.

He had worked hard doing hour after hour of overtime at the RAI archives, the place that for years kept him away from his great passions, music and painting.

He had chosen the economic security of a steady job.

He had chosen not to have problems.

He had chosen tranquility, routine.

He had chosen to be a spectator in life.

The water continued to strike on thoughts that remained impermeable to the infiltration of courage; its trickling march—oily sensation of defeat—flowed over his whole body.

Suddenly he realized he had made a mistake in all his well-considered lousy choices.

There was a fly beating against the window. It wanted to be

free — it could see freedom on the other side of the glass — but it couldn't get there.

And it was he who had put that window there with his own hands. He had constructed this prison to protect himself from a reality that he saw as unjust and crooked. He was no longer in the habit of dealing with this reality. The irony of fate was that he worked in the largest archive of documentary videos in Italy. Virtual to the nth degree. He spent hours viewing reproductions of the external world without noticing that he had ceased to inhabit the real version of the same.

Periodically he would get involved with a woman, thinking that this time around she would be the love of his life. But just as periodically he would find himself incapable of going forward with a relationship that would make it necessary for him to give up part of his own existence. Punctually he would close himself back in his own little world.

He looked at his vulnerable feet, planted on the aseptic surface of the shower floor. It was time to trample in the mud of concreteness.

Stepping out of the shower, he put on his bathrobe.

Only now did he hear Tony shouting in the bedroom. "Don't bust my balls with this bullshit!" He was on the phone. "Fine, I'll see you at three this afternoon. Prepare the papers for me to sign and tell that jerkoff that I'll pay the fines without argument. Just don't bust my balls anymore and don't use my name under any circumstances."

He must have gotten into deep shit for having interrupted the run of the play. Tony was great at getting into deep shit, but at least he lived his life to the fullest. Maybe over the top, but for sure he was not a spectator.

Tony flung open the bathroom door without knocking.

"I'm going to Rome, I'll be back in a couple of days. Try to dig up something about this Ecosystem. And don't worry, we'll figure it all out."

Without waiting for a response, he left with his duffel bag over his shoulder.

Maurizio stood still, trying to recapture the thought that had already flashed through his mind at these words.

A few seconds later he dashed over the wet floor to follow his friend. A bad idea. He fell down crying out Tony's name.

Tony, surprised by the thud and the cry, retraced his steps. He found his friend on the ground. He was holding his knee like a soccer player cut down in a counterattack.

"What's up? What have you done? At three I have a meeting with my agent."

"Listen, I've got an idea. Before you come back, can you stop by my office?"

"Yes, but why?"

"I'm going to call my colleague Angelo right now. I'll ask him to do some research on Ecosystem, hopefully we have something from the TV news. He can look at the regional coverage of Le Marche too. Whatever he finds — if he finds anything — he'll put on a DVD or flashdrive for you, okay? When you go to the office, ask for Angelo Di Pietro."

"Okay, I'll deal with it. Great! Now I'm off."

He rushed out again, leaving Maurizio still in pain on the floor, then he turned back. "Quit faking it, the referee already saw the replay."

Montegallo
Giulia Cantarini's Car
Tuesday June 19, 20XX
12:07 PM

Grim forboding. Groundless anxiety. A mysterious frustration.

Giulia was unable to explain her uneasiness. Maybe it was only simple disappointment — also very infantile. Who knows what she had expected from a mystery which turned out to be just the classic outburst of an unbalanced person. There was nothing left to find out. She had woken up to an agonizing inner emptiness. Her most immediate desire was to call her daughter, but to do that she had to get into her car and drive around until she found a cellphone signal.

She was comforted hearing the child's normal lively prattle. Nonna Lisa was a fine grandmother.

Sara's happy voice had allowed her to dive back into her work. But she didn't have anything extraordinary in hand. She continued to drive until she reached the Galluccio pass, at an altitude of 1200 meters, where she stopped the car and got out. Another clear day, with a sky swept by a north wind that tousled her hair and her thoughts. Taking advantage of these moments of grace she tried again to dig up a point of interest in a news story that was on its way to oblivion. A story on which she had bet heavily. The only element of investigative relevance that remained unexplored was the one concerning the constellation of the Virgin. Only a hypothesis, but it did lead to a further line of questioning. Was it possible that a person totally lacking in culture like Giuseppe Grossi would have known about the theory and consequently the location of the sites in question? Because if not...

In that case, you could assert the existence of an accomplice with a more evolved mind—a grey eminence—who had prompted the criminal activities. In other words, you could say that there was more to investigate.

However, the authorities were going to verify the findings. And it wasn't just that.

The investigators had no interest in prolonging an investigation that had left them impotent for twenty-four hours. Twenty-four hours in which three innocent people had died, as well as the guilty party, unsuspected until his final extreme gesture.

Montegallo and its citizens had woken up from a nightmare or, perhaps, had just been thrown into one. A neighbor above suspicion revealed as the perpetrator of atrocious crimes. After the first shock—and the media-fueled sense of dislocation and euphoria caused by being thrust into the national news limelight—they wanted to forget. They were sick of being characterized as "inhabitants of the town of horrors." Nobody except Giulia had any desire to discuss this story.

"Giuliaaa!"

An Alfa Spider pulled up next to her.

"Hello Tony. Where are you going?"

"Rome. I'll be back in a couple of days. By the way, keep an eye on Maurizio. He's acting strange."

"Worried about the house?"

"Yeah, but I don't think it's just that. It's like he's brooding about his whole life."

"Oh, don't you think you're exaggerating? I didn't know you were a psychologist."

"In fact I'm not, but I've known him since we were young. The way I see it, this place is partly to blame. It has a weird effect on me too. Ever since I got here, I keep finding myself thinking about things in ways that I haven't thought for years."

While he was talking he had gotten out of his car and approached Giulia. He lowered his voice, finding himself face to face with the object of his desire.

"Maybe you're right. After all, here we are in the magical land of the Fairy Sibyl. Actually it's got me in a bizarre state of mind, too. To think that this morning..."

He didn't let her finish the sentence. "Giulia, I'm not good at saying these things but...I...I like you...I want to say that I like you in a way different from other women...and I feel like you too..."

Giulia looked into his eyes, trying to make him understand that this was not the case, but he, caught up in his own emotions, was unable to read her gaze. He attempted the one action that, in this moment, was most inopportune.

He tried to kiss her. She drew back.

He would have vanished in a magician's trick, if only he knew one. Instead he stood there frozen, staring at the ground, his face partly covered by a few locks of hair.

"Tony, no...I think you're really nice. I have a lot of fun when I'm with you...but...at this moment in my life I'm not looking for a man. I'm sorry..."

"Excuse me...excuse me...excuse me..."

He got back in his car and took off at high speed.

The wind continued to tousle Giulia's hair and thoughts.

She realized there was something else that was bothering her.

What had happened to Morgana?

Ascoli Piceno
A Dungeon
Tuesday June 19, 20XX
1:09 PM

Anger was giving way to desperation.

They had taken away everything, including her watch, but Morgana could swear she'd been shut up here for more than twenty-four hours. Or at least, that was how much time had passed since she'd woken up with a heavy head and her memory blacked out from the moment she had sipped red wine in Count Augusto's company.

Then the darkness.

It seemed to be a cell. No window, only the dim light of a lamp. Aside from the cot, where she had slept that sleep without dreams, there was a toilet and a sink in the corner. Beyond that, absolute emptiness. Considering the humidity she had to be underground. The wooden door was never opened. A tray with a plate of white rice and a bottle of water had been passed through a low slot. But that had happened many hours earlier, and now she was hungry again.

Energy was necessary, the mental effort she was preparing would require a lot of energy. She gathered up the little that remained.

She concentrated on her surroundings, the carving in the center of the ceiling which depicted the sun with rays similar to tentacles, the sounds maybe coming from outside, the pattern of the stones making up the walls which imprisoned her. She made a mental photograph of all the details. It was the only possibility — her only hope of salvation.

Rome
Via Archimede
Mancini & Zaccardo Agency
Tuesday June 19, 20XX
3:34 PM

For the fifth time in a row, Paola Zaccardo explained that Tony's situation was defined as a breach of contract. That, in the case of non-fulfillment, the contract provided a series of penalties. The sum of which was more than 30,000 euros. That if he didn't pay up within a reasonable amount of time, the debt would triple. That, from the point of view of his career, he had to take on more work whether he wanted to or not, otherwise the agency would no longer represent him.

Tony understood, but sat silent with an absent expression that revealed to anyone looking at him his state of confusion.

He couldn't get Giulia's "No" out of his mind. Nor could he forget Maurizio's accusation of egotism.

"Tony, do you understand me? Tony!"

He heard the voice of his agent reach him from far away.

And deep down, he didn't give a shit.

"Sure, yes, yes, I understand. Now if you've finished, I'm taking off."

He got up to leave but the door was blocked by Antonella Costantini, stage name Jessica Culo, who had chosen to enter without knocking.

"Sorry to bother you Paola, but I'm in a hurry. I have to be at the club at 4:30, we're rehearsing the number with the lesbian policewomen. Tony! Darling, how are you?" Jessica wrapped herself around his neck, kissing him on the mouth. "Sweetie! It's been a hell of a long time since anybody's heard from you. Listen, call me later, tonight there's an awesome party at a wicked cool place."

"I don't know, Antonè, I'm not really in the mood. We'll do it another time."

"No, no, you gotta come. The place is called Araba Fenice and it's not just some joint, it's a villa. It's gonna be crazy fun. Call me later and I'll tell you how to get there, it's kind of out in the burbs, towards Cassia, but it's worth it."

Tony left the building, got in his car, and went home.

He telephoned Angelo Di Pietro to ask him to do some research on Ecosystem.

Then he stretched out on the bed and stared at the ceiling for three hours.

When he decided he'd had enough, he got up and made another phone call.

"Hey, Jessica!"

Montegallo
Hotel Vettore
Silvio Forlan's room
Tuesday June 19, 20XX
8:07 PM

They were already late. Silvio had been yelling at the bathroom door for a quarter of an hour while inside Simona consulted the trusted tarot cards in solitude. Ahead of them was dinner with the mayor of Montegallo. The restaurant was in an out of the way spot, chosen to not attract attention — the mayor had told him — in a place called Croce di Casale.

Simona had no desire whatsoever to go there, already anticipating a route plagued with torturous curves, just like every other tedious expedition in this harsh place reeking of hostility. She wasn't much of a nature lover, but even aside from that, she sensed, in the midst of these mountains, the looming threat of a conflict between obscure forces. Mysterious energies ready to explode in a punitive reaction against those who had for so long violated the sacred harmony of the pact decreeing mutual aid between the universe and its inhabitants.

Locked in the bathroom, she continued to stare at the three cards that lay on the toilet seat lid. She had extracted them half an hour earlier from the deck of Tarot cards — the Tower, the Devil, and the Moon.

An inauspicious premonition had assailed her all afternoon, and this really frightened her.

Ever since she was born she had known that she had special perceptions. With time she had learned to interpret these sensations, which inevitably revealed premonitions of future events; sometimes positive, sometimes negative. But now, the premonition was unbearable, a state of affliction very hard to explain even to herself. A knot of anxiety at the center of her chest with the added punch to the stomach delivered by those three cards dealt out in an anonymous bathroom in an anonymous hotel room.

The Tower, the Devil, and the Moon: an accursed combination tied to the most occult and malevolent of human inclinations. Over the centuries human beings had developed their own wickedness, and Evil had always helped them pursue ambitions and aims that otherwise would have been too difficult to achieve.

She looked out the window. The sharp peak of Mt. Vettore looked like a knife pointed towards the blue and innocent sky. It was a merciless and honest contrast, so different from the hypocrisy of the human condition.

"Simonaaa! It's late, shit! We have to go!"

Yes, it was late, maybe it was already too late.

Also for her, who had chosen the shortcut to easy wealth by staying with a man she had never loved.

The king of mineral water, whose conscience was polluted by the most banal of vices.

Greed.

Montegallo
Village of Astorara
Maurizio Verdimani's House
Tuesday June 19, 20XX
9:32 PM

A perfect dinner with a delightful and unexpected guest, Giulia Cantarini.

The reporter had followed up on Tony's request, knocking on Maurizio's door partly because she was bored and partly to atone for having rejected her clumsy suitor's kiss.

The master of the house, initially taken by surprise, had overcome his embarrassment by challenging himself to make a classic spaghetti all'Amatriciana. Heartened by the excellent results, he added a good bottle of red wine,

Then he let himself go in the pleasure of her company.

It was Giulia who uncorked the second bottle.

The journalist related that she had asked her paper for information on Ecosystem and they would let her know the results. In addition she had made an appointment for him the next day with a lawyer that a co-worker had recommended.

For what it mattered, the lawyer loved the mountains and was well acquainted with the area around Montegallo.

To Giulia, Maurizio was a real discovery. She had noticed right away the paintings hung on the walls, and when she asked who had created them, the answer was very unexpected.

"Are they that ugly? What can I say, painting has always been my passion."

"But what are you saying? They're beautiful!"

The style recalled Chagall in the colors, the lines, the settings, and in the chosen subjects: human figures suspended in domestic interiors turned upside-down, fantastic animals in flight over surreal landscapes in vivid and unnatural colors. Red skies, blue mountains, young women holding hands with winged lovers, anthropomorphic beasts tinted with shades of a tormented soul.

A sort of dream world, a world turned on its head, a world

seen through colored glass. A hodgepodge of innocent purity and profound poetry. All of it pervaded by a childlike melancholy.

Or perhaps not, maybe they weren't that beautiful. Maybe the special appreciation that she felt for these paintings resulted from the unexpected discovery of a man who, up until now, had seemed like the most anonymous of office workers. A man now revealed as being full of creativity and charm, both traits closed up inside of a complex personality, difficult to interpret.

Giulia listened, swept away by the river of words pouring from the handsome mouth framed by the well-tended black goatee that Maurizio had kept the same length for more than twenty years.

The eloquence unleashed by the second bottle of wine had launched the archivist into an unprecedented autobiographical tale. Chapter: Music.

Giulia smiled, asked a few questions, and touched her hair.

One of Tony's many lessons on picking up girls, unrequested but given anyway, popped into Maurizio's mind. "When a woman looks at you, laughs, and touches her hair, it's a done deal. You have to kiss her right away!"

He had no intention of trying to seduce the lovely journalist. Not because he didn't like her. On the contrary, he thought she was splendid, but the burst of lightheartedness that the woman had brought to these hours was good enough. He certainly didn't want to ruin everything with an awkward advance.

And then there was Tony. His friend was very attracted to her, he had never seen the guy so taken, so interested.

In any case, given the pleasure he felt riding this wave of euphoric affinity, he fell back on a tactic he always relied on in special moments with a beautiful girl.

"Wait."

Giulia remained motionless. Silently she watched him rise from his seat and head with a slouching gait towards the next room. In a few seconds he came back with a guitar in hand.

He returned to sit in front of her, looking her in the eyes, smiling like an excited child, and began to play. His fingers moved nimbly over the strings.

He began to sing.

"Un uomo onesto, un uomo probo, tralallala... tralallallero, si innamorò perdutamente di una che non l'amava niente..."

Giulia knew this song very well, "La Ballata dell'Amore Cieco" — "The Ballad of Blind Love" — by De Andrè.

When he had finished, the surprised minstrel was showered with warm applause and an even more pleasing exhortation, "More! Another one!"

And so he went on.

There followed a hit parade interspersed with a series of glasses filled from the third bottle of the evening.

"More, more..."

Maurizio Verdimani was transformed into a human juke box. On request he offered up the desired song: a revival dedicated above all to Fabrizio de Andre and Rino Gaetano, with digressions into Lucio Battisti, in which Giulia Cantarini participated as vocalist.

Right in the middle of "Motocicletta... dieci HP... tutta cromata... e tua se dici siiii..." the loud rumble of a motor shattered the mood.

They went to the window and saw the usual black truck climbing toward the hills followed by two more.

After a few seconds the night became silent again and full of stars. Maurizio explained what had just happened.

"Every night, right around this time, a black truck goes by headed up towards the area of the landslide. I don't know what..."

He didn't finish the phrase because Giulia kissed him.

Rome
Villa Araba Fenice
Tuesday June 19, 20XX
11:47 PM

Seven lines of white powder on a plate set on the bedside table to the left of the bed.

This is what Tony saw when he rolled over after freeing himself from the voluptuous embrace of a beautiful woman with a mane of ruffled red hair and a twisted expression. She had been licking his nipple. He didn't remember her name so he accompanied his movement with a generic "Excuse me, dear."

Sitting up and reaching towards the plate, he became aware of the presence of the other woman who had followed him, along with the redhead, into one of the many available bedrooms. She continued to writhe between his legs while frantically touching between her own. With her mouth she lightly stroked his numb semi-hard dick.

She had smooth black hair, and was watching him while she licked the tip of his thing with her tongue. Her eyes were prisoners of an insupportable solitude, the raven locks barred pupils filled with empty seduction. He couldn't remember this one's name either. He extricated himself with an aseptic "Wait a second," and picked up the plate, under which he found a tightly rolled twenty euro banknote. Raising the plate with one hand, he put the little cylinder up his right nostril with the other.

He took a hit.

He passed the plate and the banknote to the two women. Then he attacked a half-full bottle of Jack Daniel's he found on the floor next to the bed.

Smiling with satisfaction, he was able to remember that he had put it there. Something, anyway, that he could still remember.

He stood up and looked in the mirror. Like his two companions, he was naked. That was good. He took his cock in his hand and began to jerk off, trying to get it erect.

He couldn't take his eyes off the scene. Three nude bodies reflected in a big mirror sending back a vision — more than the banal exhibition of flesh — of vacant gazes lost in the desire for enjoyment.

Tony wanted to turn off his brain, he wanted to lose himself, to degenerate in a mental brothel where he could bury the reality that awaited him the next day beyond the walls of the Villa Araba Fenice. In order to ensure the achievement of this result he had purchased fifteen grams of cocaine. Three bags of five. The first was almost finished. He had offered it to the two women, to his friend Jessica, to the bartender, and to a trans who Jessica had introduced as the director of the place. He had snorted with everyone.

The more he snorted, the more whiskey and vodka he drank.

As always, he was astonished by how much the gentle sex was attracted to cocaine. The women who had this vice were real vacuum cleaners, and every time they'd snorted it, they revealed themselves as starved for sex.

In fact the redhead had gotten a foot-long dildo out of a drawer and was using it with meticulous zeal on the appropriate zone of the brunette. This one gave clear signs of enjoyment, emphasizing everything with moans and beatific glances, all reflected in a mirror that resembled ever more closely the screen of a pornographic movie house from the '80's.

The sensation of ridiculous and squalid perdition pleased Tony, originating in the innermost scorn he also felt for himself, for his soul polluted with the incapacity to live.

What he sought was oblivion.

The door opened. The three were completely undisturbed. In a place like this it was nothing unusual, in fact it could be a lovely surprise.

It was Jessica Culo. Half naked.

"Looking good! Tony, I gotta ask you a favor."

Tony was having trouble uttering any words. However, he demonstrated an affectionate availability by coming close and sticking his tongue in her mouth. Jessica understood that she had his attention.

"Tony, I've got this friend. He's a bigwig, a Senator. Well, it's like this, he likes the...you understand...but he's all out, 'cuz he only got a little, but see, it would be a fucking great thing...and he'd pay good."

Tony, while listening, drank. After he had drained the bottle of whiskey, he tried to express the few ideas that he had succeeded in dragging out of his brain as it whirled into the void.

"Listen, I'm really not into selling the shit. If you want...you can come in here with us...That way the Senator can help himself to the plate he'll find by chance on the bedside table...But just you two..."

Montegallo
Provincial Road 67
Towards Propezzano, a Village in Montegallo
Silvio Forlan's Car
Wednesday June 20, 20XX
12:13 AM

"Can you believe that asshole? He wanted to get paid in full! Worse than an accountant. But if we don't get the concession by Thursday, I'm going to go apeshit. I swear I'll rip him a new one."

Simona heard without listening, accustomed as she was to the plaintive tirades of the executioner who, to ease his guilty conscience, always tried to make himself look better by blaming the victim.

"I don't understand how a man like that could be elected by the great majority of his district. An ignorant shopkeeper who demands his own personal cut as if it was a right! And who looks at you as if you were the only crook, who's corrupting him, when he's the one shaking you down for a wad of cash!"

Simona heard without listening, luxuriating in the sensation of well-being that she could never have imagined a few hours earlier. The evil omens had proved to be baseless. She had dined well, and now she even enjoyed the twisty curves, observing the starry heavens through the skylight of the car.

Forlan drove, talking, glaring at the windshield. "You know what I'm going to do now? I'm going to call that asshole Cecchini. He's gonna pay!"

He extracted his phone from his pocket, hit a couple of buttons, waited.

"The jerk isn't answering."

He tried again. This time it went better.

Rome
Villa Araba Fenice
Wednesday June 20, 20XX
12:24 AM

Senator Emidio Cecchini made his entrance wearing only his pants. He had his jacket, shirt and tie in one hand, his shoes and underwear in the other.

The ring of a cellphone cut short the honorable Senator's effusively polite greeting. "Excuse me, I have to answer this, it's important." Setting his shoes and underwear on the floor, he fished his cellphone out the jacket pocket, and cleared his throat. "Hello…"

He retreated to a corner of the room, but it was an animated conversation, and he didn't always succeed in muffling his words.

Tony, along with the redhead, the brunette, and Jessica, was sprawled on the bed, desiring only to recapture his descent into the sensual limbo, but he was distracted by various fragments of the discussion Cecchini was engaged in.

At first he thought he heard wrong, but with an enormous effort of concentration, he pricked up his ears and understood the unthinkable.

The Senator was talking about Montegallo, about water, about a mayor who had demanded a bribe.

Shit! Montegallo, water, mayor!

He passed the plate without taking a snort. He left the bed to look for the unopened bottle of vodka he'd set on the table when he had entered the room at the beginning of the evening. One gulp was enough to counter the effects of the coke and regain a small spark of lucidity.

That was better—or maybe he only thought so—anyway, good enough to figure out the next step. Going over to his pants and getting out a pack of cigarettes, he grabbed his cellphone as well. He activated the video function, setting it to take a panoramic shot of the whole scene with as much of the sound as possible. The apparatus had to perch on a corner of the small table, next to objects placed at the disposition of whoever might want to liven up encounters with bodies that had inevitably become boring. He decided to lean it up against the shaft of a dildo, on the tip of which, instead of the head of the dick, was the form of a closed fist. In another context, it might have been taken to be a souvenir from a communist country, perhaps the reproduction of an obelisk celebrating the glorious party. But in this context it was easy to guess what its mission was. He had to smile: who even knew what the Senator's political party was? Not that he would ever ask. With a little cunning he would try to quiz him about other things. If—as he thought—the Senator had a weakness for coke, it shouldn't be hard.

- -

Montegallo
Provincial Road 67
Village of Propezzano
Silvio Forlan's Car
Wednesday June 20, 20XX
12:33 AM

"Cecchini, you're really busting my balls! Enough with the gossip, I want the facts. And I want them right away. Goodbye."

He hadn't said anything new to the Senator, but nonetheless he felt that he had asserted his leadership, showing the determination which always forced human beings to submit.

Except for Simona Coda, naturally. She could not care less about his determination.

"I have to make him listen up, like always. You can't back down in this life, you can't give an inch, especially to those asshole politicians. That Cecchini's a fucking idiot, but this time I'm going to rip him to shreds...him and Assergi..."

Simona heard but didn't listen, distracted as she was by the crescent moon that hung, luminous, overhead.

Heard but didn't listen. She hadn't listened for a long time, distracted as she was by the necessity of making sense of her own existence, by her inability to explain the reasons for many mistaken choices, including living with someone she detested.

"I don't trust those pieces of shit. Especially that phony innocent Assergi."

Heard but didn't listen, distracted as she was...

"Stop!!!"

In the middle of the deserted road a crosswise car blocked their lane. Forlan, startled by the cry, braked. The headlights lit up the figure of an individual waving his arms energetically, signaling them to stop.

"What the fuck is this?"

"Wait! Don't you see he needs help?

Forlan lowered his window.

The man fired two pistol shots into his head.

Rome
Villa Araba Fenice
Wednesday June 20, 20XX
2:39 AM

Lady T joined the group.

Cecchini was particularly appreciative. After he'd vacuumed up a little of that white powder his cock was, as usual, miniaturized. However, he had discovered other pleasures. The trans had his back while he tried to regain the esteem of the three damsels by frantically using his tongue and hands.

Tony had ceased to be interested in the sex and the various other forms of perdition. A new light had switched on in his brain, with a concrete objective, a redeeming goal to pursue. For more than an hour he dedicated himself to looking after the Senator, profiting from the extraordinary comradeship that always sprang up between cokeheads. A confidential rapport blossomed between them.

For Emidio Cecchini, this good Samaritan, whose name he didn't even remember, was transformed into his best friend for life. He relaxed, abandoning himself to the frenetic dialogue, opening his heart. He talked about everything.

Tony recorded it all.

At a certain moment the actor decided it was time to leave the stage. Viewing this scene from the outside made him laugh and at the same time he felt ridiculous. Up until the entrance of the illustrious guest, he had occupied the place of honor on the bed. Of course with certain differences...

Anyway he was ready to get going. He wanted to return to Montegallo as quickly as possible with this present for Giulia. The reporter would definitely be pleased with the disclosures of the Senator regarding the shady deals between the mayor and the entrepreneur of mineral water. The first citizen had sold the most precious resource of his community; the price was right only for the one involved. A bribe of 50,000 euros. The same amount would definitely have gone to the parliamentarian, who, even if he was acting like a clown, took great care not to the mention the particulars.

While dressing he noticed he was especially rumpled, both in his clothing and his physique. He needed to stop by his house to take a shower, after which he would hit the road.

Montegallo
Marshal Moser's Quarters
Wednesday June 20, 20XX
4:52 AM

Francesco Moser, with his back against the headboard, the bedside light on, and a brain incapable of repose, let his gaze run for a moment over his wife's extended body.

Her regular breathing made him think of serene sleep.

That night he was immune to any such torpor.

For hours he had been re-reading Prof. Roiati's book, which discussed in great detail the thesis of the churches situated in a mode to replicate Virgo.

The places that the four corpses had been found corresponded to four of the sites described in the book. To think that it was only a coincidence would be absurd.

But what did it mean?

The telephone rang.

Gilda sat bolt upright in bed. Even though she was a Carabiniere's wife, she wasn't used to sudden news in the middle of the night. In the fifteen years she'd spent with her husband in Monte-gallo nothing had ever happened.

Francesco held the receiver to his ear; his face was ashen.

On the other end was the lance corporal Marucci. "Marshal, are you listening? Hello, can you hear me?"

"Yes yes, go ahead."

"...so, we stopped because the car was empty, but there were visible traces of blood. After reconnoitering the zone, we found the two corpses, a man and a woman. The persons in question are Silvio Forlan, the king of mineral water, and his companion Simona Coda."

"Tell me again, where exactly?"

"Inside the little church of Santa Maria delle Grazie, in Cornaloni, at the edge of Propezzano. But the most disturbing thing is the state in which the bodies were found, at least one of the two, the woman's."

"What about it?"

"It's headless. The woman was decapitated after she was killed with two pistol shots to the chest, while the man was shot in the face. Two shots for him too. We found the woman's head inside the church. Marshal, are you still there?"

"Of course I'm still here, what the hell! I'm listening, finish what you're saying!"

"Okay...the head was on the altar, and it had been opened..."

"What do you mean opened?"

"Well, opened...the top of the skull cap had been removed in order to extract a gland. Wait a minute because maybe I wrote it down wrong, I'll ask the doctor who's here..."

"But what the hell are you..."

"Okay. The pineal gland. P-I-N-E-A-L gland. Do you under-stand me?"

"And where is this gland now?"

"Well, it's not here."

Montegallo
A Bedroom
Wednesday June 20, 20XX
6:47 AM

A dream. It was only a dream. Strange, terrifying, realistic.

Giulia opened her eyes wide. She shuddered. The sensations she'd just been feeling continued to course through her, confusing her perceptions of reality.

She remembered it well.

She remembered the dark. There weren't any windows, just one door. Everything around her was stone. Nothing else but stone.

She also remembered the cold, the white tunic too thin to protect her from the damp in the narrow cell, and she remembered the noise. A low and uninterrupted roar, a river probably.

It was flowing from someplace not far away.

Finally, the fear. Fear not just of what she had felt, but for how she had felt it. As if she were another person.

Morgana. Or actually, Morgana and Giulia at the same time. Two heads, two bodies, two souls united by the same consciousness. By the same piercing fear.

She had screamed.

She had woken up.

She realized she was still hearing the pounding — it was real.

Someone was knocking at the door.

Montegallo
Astorara
Maurizio Verdimani's House
Wednesday June 20, 20XX
6:50 AM

When Maurizio finally opened the door, he saw Tony raising his fist to pound yet again.

"About time! I've been out here for half an hour. Listen, I have a ton of things to tell you!"

He didn't give Maurizio a chance to respond. Entering the house and letting his duffel bag fall to the floor, he began to empty his pockets: his cellphone, a flash drive, five mini-bottles of vodka, two DVD's and little bag of white powder. He hadn't stopped talking. "So I decided to make kind of a wild night of it. I did some shopping, you understand, right? Shopping! Then I went to hook up with Jessica Culo, and guess who I met there? Guess! Come on, guess who I met!"

"But how the fuck should I know? It's six in the morning! You're fried on coke, and I'm fucking pissed off!"

"Listen, I'm clear as a bell. I had to take another couple of hits to stay awake, but I swear that I know what I'm saying..."

He told Maurizio about his encounter with the Senator, the business with the water, the corruption of the mayor, that he'd taped everything and how he had left in a hurry to tell him and Giulia everything.

Above all, Giulia. In fact, he wanted go and find her now, to give her the whole story.

"Good morning."

They turned around.

Wrapped up in a too large white bathrobe, with one foot still in Maurizio's bedroom, Giulia Cantarini made her appearance.

Montegallo
Astorara
Maurizio Verdimani's House
Wednesday June 20, 20XX
6:59 AM

Tony collapsed into the first chair he found.

Suddenly, the light of day became unbearable. His head was too heavy. Ideas rattled against the walls of a brain exhausted by alkaloid substances. He closed his eyelids, floating for a few seconds in an empty darkness, then ran his hands through his hair and turned back to look at Maurizio and Giulia. He felt tired. Tired and ridiculous. The whole situation seemed ridiculous, to the point of making him laugh.

Maurizio kept quiet. He would have liked to talk but he realized that this wasn't the moment. His friend's laughter, a little hysterical, made him understand that any attempt to explain would be useless and extremely embarrassing.

Giulia didn't come up with anything either. Basically there was nothing to say.

Tony headed for the stairs.

"I'm wiped out. I have to sleep."

More knocking on the door.

"Now who's that?"

It seemed excessive when Marshal Moser's now familiar voice sounded outside.

Tony had succumbed to his longing for bed without waiting to discover the identity of the new guest.

"Good morning," Moser said to Maurizio when he opened the door." "I'm looking for Signora Cantarini. I didn't find her at home, so I thought I might find her here. And in fact her car is outside..." He seemed very agitated. "Listen to me closely. Last night two more people were killed. We thought that everything was over, that the perpetrator was that madman Giuseppe Grossi. Instead, now someone's killed Silvio Forlan and his companion Simona Coda. And do you know where we found the two bodies?"

Full of curiosity, Giulia examined his face, drained by stress and lack of sleep. It wasn't like him to be giving out so much information.

"In the church of Santa Maria delle Grazie at Propezzano, one of the churches of the constellation of the Virgin. Do you see? It's possible — even probable, in my opinion — that the killer is following a very specific route. Officially, my superiors, above all the magistrate, don't want to hear any discussion of this. But only officially. In fact, at this point we're dealing with the only real clue, which we can't possibly reveal to the press."

Maurizio was about to shit in his pants.

He realized that Tony had left everything on the table, including the little baggie of white powder. Crap, there must be at least five grams of cocaine!

For the moment, the marshal seemed to be more concerned with speaking his mind than with looking around.

Giulia was entranced. By now awake and with her senses alert, she activated all her cerebral synapses in one direction. The situation was more wide open than ever. The exclusive book deal was still possible.

"So Marshal, if I understand you correctly . . . you've come to ask me to keep quiet regarding the theory of the constellation of the Virgin, since I'm the only one who knows about it, right?"

"Not just you. Your two friends have to keep their mouths shut too. You have to adhere to the official version issued by the magistrate, in which no mention is made of any connection with the other homicides. It only reports a double murder resulting from an attempted robbery gone bad. But above all I need to talk to an expert who can keep this completely under wraps. So I thought, who better than your friend, Morgana Bucci? After all, the book was found in her house. According to my information, she's considered one of the major local experts on this stuff."

Maurizio pretended to be following this discussion, but in reality he was trying to find a casual way to stretch his hand over the white packet. Giulia had the opposite reaction; nothing could have attracted her attention more than those words.

"There's a problem . . ."

"What problem? We have to analyze the motives that drive the killer, or killers, to choose these places to commit the crimes. Our experts agree that we might be dealing with ritual sacrifices. If we succeed in interpreting these rituals, we may be able to figure out the next potential crime scene. At this point, it's logical to think that the killer wants to complete the map."

"Yes, but . . ."

"No 'buts.' We have to understand the reasoning, foresee the movements. Only that way do we have the possibility of setting a trap."

Finally she was able to interrupt him. "Marshal, the problem is that Morgana Bucci has disappeared!"

Maurizio took advantage of the marshal's momentary perplexity to cover the baggie with the palm of his hand. He let it fall onto the chair between his legs. His t-shirt and boxers had no pockets.

Giulia explained about the note that Morgana had left and the fact that her cellphone was disconnected. She didn't know how to contact her friend, who lived alone and didn't have any family that she was aware of.

She asked Moser if he could trace the Count Piloni de Castris; they had apparently gone away together. She didn't have the courage, however, to recount her dream, the distressing feeling that kept her company during the night in which Morgana had vanished.

Moser agreed. In the meantime, if she could take a look at the book and do some research on the matter of the churches…since she had access to Morgana Bucci's library. Besides, the fact that she herself wanted to write a book provided an incentive. "Because you're still interested in the exclusive, right?"

"Of course I'm interested!"

"Understand that there are important details we haven't revealed yet, for obvious reasons. But if you help me, you'll have all the information as soon as possible. All right, then, let's do it like this. You'll come to the station now and I'll give you a copy of the reports relative to last night's murders. Then we'll go together to Signora Bucci's house and try to come up with an idea of what this psycopath's reasoning is. Until we locate Signora Bucci, you'll be my consultant. Naturally, the fundamental condition is that you maintain absolute silence until the conclusion of the investigation."

"I'm with you."

She rushed into the room where she had passed the night. In a minute she had gathered up her clothes strewn on the floor.

Moser used that minute to remind Signor Verdimani of the importance of confidentiality on the part of himself and his friend as well.

Maurizio swore absolute secrecy. When Giulia returned, ready to go, he got to his feet to say goodbye, but more importantly, to get rid of the Carabiniere as soon as possible. Those five grams of coke made him extremely nervous.

Suddenly, a dull sound. The house began to tremble. The furniture danced. Two glasses fell to the ground and broke into a thousand pieces. The three tried to go outside, but there wasn't enough time. The earthquake tremor was over.

The packet of cocaine had also fallen to the floor. Nobody noticed.

They looked at each other, savoring for a few seconds the pleasing immobility of the floor.

When the marshal and Giulia had gone, Maurizio picked up the drug to throw it away, but then he thought better.

Going into Tony's room, he placed it on the bedside table.

The actor hadn't noticed anything.

He was sleeping on his back, with his mouth wide open, snoring.

Ascoli Piceno
A Dungeon
Wednesday June 20, 20XX
9:07 AM

White rice again. Tap water again. The sliding wooden panel had been slammed shut with an extraordinary vigor, as if the unknown jailer was feeling ever more impatient serving the hostage. Or maybe this impression was due to the weariness that now filled her. Especially after the effort she'd exerted to contact Giulia, the only friend crazy enough to understand the nature of her request.

Morgana ate the rice and drank the water. Once again she held fast to the clear idea of feeding and hydrating herself, to withstand as much as possible while awaiting the next development in an already terrifying situation.

She didn't understand why. Why was she here? In what way was the Count involved in her kidnapping? That the aristocrat was behind this whole nightmare was a certainty at this point. The last image fixed in her mind was Augusto's face in the grips of a mystical exposition about the Sibillini water, the female divinities, the four elements, and other esoteric concepts, an absurd cocktail of delirious ravings.

The sudden clanging of the lock caught Morgana in the midst of her meal and her reconstruction of those last minutes in her house at Corbara.

For the first time since she had been imprisoned, the door opened. A little bit at a time, with exasperating slowness, a hooded form dressed in white made his entrance.

The Master! Or at least he seemed like the same person the guests had hailed at that strange gathering she'd been invited to a week earlier. She also recognized the medallion.

"Tomorrow you will leave this place," he said after staring at her for a long time. "We will go to the most sacred site of the Brotherhood of the Oracles."

Morgana didn't respond. She was concentrating more than ever on trying to understand what he had in mind.

"Tomorrow at 12:26 exactly the summer solstice will occur. You know what that signifies, true?"

She knew it well. The Sun, symbol of divine fire, would enter into the constellation of Cancer, symbol of the waters ruled by the Moon. In the meeting and the union of the two opposing polarities — the male side and the female side — the male side, the Sun, would achieve his maximum positive inclination.

Symbolically, the phenomena was represented by a six-pointed star, uniting the triangle of Fire and the triangle of Water.

"You will be the protagonist in a ritual of fundamental importance for me and for all of the Brotherhood. There will also be an unexpected gift from another woman, like you a repository of the gift of clairvoyance — her third eye. Along with yours, it will be raised onto the most sacred of altars and then absorbed with the help of the sacred waters."

Morgana was paralyzed by a flood of freezing panic.

She had understood what her destiny was to be.

She had definitely recognized the gaze of her jailer.

She had become aware that the Count Piloni de Castris, at 12:26 PM of the next day, would decapitate her. He would then extract the pineal gland from her head and he would eat it.

She didn't say anything.

Ascoli Piceno
Office of the Lawyer Bonanni
Wednesday June 20, 20XX
11:34 AM

"You see, Signor Verdimani, Ecosystem is a very important company on an international level, one of the few of that status with an office in Ascoli Piceno. It seems strange to me that they would have committed any technical or legal errors. In any case, I'll investigate everything carefully and let you know." With his plump fingers Cesare Bonanni touched the papers that Maurizio had given him, placing in the lawyer's hands his hope of finding a way out of his obsession.

"Montegallo is a marvelous place. I'm very fond of the mountains, did you know?" Bonanni punctuated his words with a polite smile that annoyed the archivist. "I know the area well, in the past I went there often, especially in the summer — the trails, the villages, the beautiful mountains... I also know Astorara..."

A mist of white spit appeared every so often on those thin lips that Maurizio couldn't stop staring at, as they presented a sequence of observations delivered like a nursery rhyme.

"Usually we've stayed at the Albergo Vettore, but for the last two years my wife and I have rented a cottage in one of the villages."

While talking he continued to examine the documents, leafing through them with the habitual gestures of someone who was never surprised by any detail.

"You know, I specialize in legal issues dealing with minors. Over the years I have preferred to occupy myself more and more with problems involving children and young people... I find it more useful... more stimulating. However, don't worry, that's merely a preference. To tell the truth I have the honor of being highly regarded here in the city, and therefore I'm accustomed to being consulted on every type of question."

He paused to look at a photograph of the front of the disputed house. At that moment the secretary announced the presence of Signora Bonanni who, without any further formalities, appeared in the office.

Maurizio took advantage of her entrance. He said goodbye to the lawyer, telling him that he would be awaiting any news.

His main desire was to get out of there as quickly as possible.

Montegallo
Village of Balzo
Mayor's Office
Wednesday June 20, 20XX
3:22 PM

The walls shook.

The windowpanes rattled.

The desk lurched.

A sheaf of paper, a stapler, a calculator and two pens fell to the floor.

Mayor Assergi anchored himself to the couch. Dr. Mascetti, the town secretary, also in the office at that moment, succeeded in uttering only one very intelligent word. "Earthquake!"

Intense tremors, even though brief. Or at least that's how it seemed to both of them. They were accustomed to living in what the TV news programs defined as "the seismic zone of Central Italy." It was the third tremor of the day. The experts were expecting more.

Mascetti was the first to take a breath. "The only bright side of this damn earthquake is that it will distract the press."

Assergi pulled the desk back into position. "Yeah, but still it's a nuisance, as well as a potential danger. We'll have to make sure right away that there hasn't been any damage to people or houses."

"I'll go organize the civil defense team."

"Do me a favor, see to it we come off looking good."

The secretary was about to leave, but he was called back from the door.

"Another thing: cancel the debate on the concession of the springs to Acque Sane. Forlan, poor soul, he can't do anything with them now. And call Marshal Moser. I want to see him."

Montegallo
Village of Corbara
Morgana Bucci's House
7:47 PM

The big table was covered with documents: records, evaluations, and photographs from the files that Giulia had gotten from Marshal Moser. Statements written in a dry bureaucratic language but terrifying in their content, autopsy reports aseptic in their description but pitiless in their significance, images of death lacking any elements of consolation. The volumes taken from Morgana's library and the reporter's laptop completed the landscape that she had laid out on the ample walnut table during these hours of fruitless research. Giulia dedicated herself first to the reading of the reports of the investigators, then to the determination of possible ties between the blood-soaked events and the occult practices that made up part of the traditions and legends of the Sibillini.

She knew by heart the details of the crimes committed up until the apparent suicide of Giuseppe Grossi.

Now it could only be defined in that way: apparent.

The latest development was the execution of Forlan and his companion Simona Coda. The double murder showed the existence of a criminal will that went beyond the theory of the scapegoat stricken on the road to repentance, of the poor uncouth ignorant victim of a past trauma who had killed himself in a moment of clearly admitted guilt. One had to think of a wider plan in which the placement of the bodies represented a precise intention on the part of the killer or killers. This placement provided an evident connection between all the murders and in consequence gave rise to the suspicion that Giuseppe Grossi had been killed, or had even been induced to kill himself.

But what eluded her was the motive. Why all these crimes? Maybe for the water? She didn't know. Certainly water played a major role in all these obscure happenings given the words traced with the first victim's blood — the warning of the killer — and the last double crime, in which one of those killed was the entrepreneur who wanted to exploit the precious resource. But what did the water of Montegallo have to do with the churches dedicated to the Virgin? Churches that, according to an esoteric theory, were built there in homage to the myth of the Sibyl, and therefore to the female divinity. Beyond that, why so much violence to Simona Coda's corpse, whose pineal gland had been removed? In the last hour she had concentrated all her attention on this horrifying new detail — arriving at an interesting discovery.

In the supernatural world, the pineal gland corresponded to the omniscient third eye, the eye that sees everything. Reactivating it was one of the primary aims of various types of meditation. While consulting an old text regarding certain divinatory practices, she found herself facing information that was, to say the least, curious.

The pineal gland produces DMT, a substance able to carry the individual on voyages beyond time and space. This happens at night, while dreaming, during the period when the pineal gland is most active. The ever lesser importance which human beings attributed to the third eye had led to the gradual atrophy of the organ. That wasn't all. Water flows inside the pineal gland, water that over time calcifies. In this process of calcification could be found the principle cause of atrophy: therefore it was necessary to decalcify the gland in order to reactivate it. Such a result could be achieved at night, with darkness, with sleep, and with specific meditative techniques, but above all, with the daily consumption of water whose magical properties were opportunely strengthened by the mysterious formulas of the ancients.

By regaining control of the gland, one obtained the gift of reading the future and divining the destiny of human beings. In sum, the possibility of wielding boundless power.

Giulia Cantarini felt she had picked out the thread that, however unbelievable, tied together all the events of these days.

Hypothesizing the existence of a fanatic of occultism, or even more than one — of a sect, for example — would explain the morbid interest in the water of a land that for millennia had been the legendary setting of fairies, witches, sorcerers and, above all, the unequaled oracle, the Sibyl. The conviction that, by way of special spells, this water could bestow the gift of predicting the future might have led someone to kill, to prevent the precious element from ending up in the hands of a vulgar merchant.

The merchant is dead; the water has been saved.

This line of thinking made a certain amount of sense.

But why remove poor Simona Coda's pineal gland, and only hers? The perpetrator of the double homicide must not be the same person who had committed the first crimes. The investigators had attributed the first ones to Giuseppe Grossi, but Giulia continued to be perplexed about that. Re-reading the index card regarding Simona Coda, she was struck by the fact that the victim had been well-known for her history of occult sensitivities. In this role she had often been a guest on TV programs, a media career she had interrupted to be with Silvio Forlan.

In any case, nothing. Nothing came into her mind.

She had not succeeded in finding a logical and concrete reason for the mutilation inflicted by a psychopath. Because it could only be the work of a psychopath.

Better stop for a minute, think about something else, something totally different.

She was seized with the desire to see her daughter's smile, the intelligent gaze of her adorable little girl.

She rapidly tapped on the keys of her laptop.

Looking for the file that collected the family photos, she clicked on the wrong thing. Instead of Sara's face, what appeared on the screen were the images from her special report on the restoration of Forte Malatesta.

She had taken many pictures for that piece of propaganda in favor of the city administration, pandering in the name of art.

The old holding cells provided a merciless vision of the suffering undergone by the prisoners during the whole period, up to the 1970's, in which the fort had been a prison.

Suddenly she felt the same unease again that had struck her on entering some of these little rooms, with walls made of stone that, no matter how often they were cleaned, seemed to preserve the agonizing desire for liberty of whose who had dwelt within.

The same sensation as the dream.

The same stones!

A shiver ran down her spine.

She scrutinized the photos that portrayed the details of the cells, to validate her identification of the stones. She recognized one in particular, set in the center of the ceiling and sculpted to represent the sun. She recognized too, the wooden door.

Her own thoughts astounded and frightened her.

The dream could only be a call for help from Morgana. Her friend, locked in one of the cells in the Forte Malatesta, had launched a desperate SOS in the only way available, a way only she knew.

But Giulia, what could she possibly do? She didn't know.

If she called the police they would laugh in her face. The Forte Malatesta hadn't reopened yet, the work site hadn't shut down. Access was restricted to the workers and was supervised by the city officials of Ascoli Piceno.

She could try to track down Marshal Moser. No! She didn't want to look ridiculous.

She could go take a look. By herself. If she noticed something suspicious, then she would call the police.

Getting into her car, she looked at the dashboard clock with the illuminated date. Forte Malatesta would reopen in three days. For the occasion, the city of Ascoli Piceno had organized an exhibit dedicated to the inventions of Leonardo Da Vinci. Opening Saturday June 23. "Faithful reproductions realized by woodworkers from all over Italy," proclaimed the slogan she had read in the press release furnished by an employee of the administration; she still had Dr. Antonini's telephone number with her. She would call him as soon as possible, but first she had to find reception for her cellphone.

She pressed her foot down on the accelerator.

Montegallo
Village of Astorara
Maurizio Verdimani's House
Wednesday June 20, 20XX
8:14 PM

Tony woke up depressed and pissed off, as usual after a long night of drugs and sex.

This time however he felt even more distressed, even more discouraged.

There was the same old guilt, but this time doubled. It wasn't just for his eternal throwing away of his life, for his repeated dives to the bottom — a bottom he was driven to touch so that he could rise up, once more proving to himself his great strength — but also because he had embarrassed Maurizio and Giulia without having any right to do so.

Making things difficult for someone close to you because of your own weakness was, for Tony and his ego, unacceptable.

It was early afternoon when he got out of bed, with his head full of confused reasoning and exaggerated common sense.

He was hungry as a wolf.

Obviously. He hadn't eaten for more than thirty-six hours.

In the kitchen he scrounged up some food. Full of new energy, he felt ready to fix whatever he had totally fucked up.

But what had he totally fucked up? He wasn't in any condition to create any total fuck-ups! The total fuck-ups were all in his head. The only total fuck-up was himself.

In any case he wanted to make things right.

Rebuild his friendship with Maurizio from the foundation up.

Leave Giulia with good memories of him and then exit the scene with a sweep of his cloak. An elegant and unforgettable way to say Adieu...Farewell...Addio...to one whom he had loved, without being loved in return.

He wanted to behave as a gentleman towards both of them.

Yes, but...

If Maurizio had conquered this fascinating woman's heart, perhaps the credit was also a little his, for his advice, his lessons...

For the thousandth time in his life he made himself return to the good intentions he'd laid down to cleanse his soul of the demons that tormented him.

Okay! He would start with Giulia, because Maurizio wasn't at home. Tony had called his cellphone, full of embarrassment, but as usual his friend had been extremely civil and rational. In a cool tone he had informed Tony that he would be walking around Ascoli for a while after he talked with the lawyer that Giulia had recommended. He had added that the reporter had stayed in Montegallo, busy studying the case that Moser had dropped off in the morning, and that later he would explain everything. The important thing was that Tony shouldn't talk about it with anybody. Tony had agreed to this without understanding at all.

Returning to his bedroom he got dressed. While looking for his car keys he took stock of the diverse array of objects present on the bedside table.

The flash drive and the two DVD's went back in the outer pocket of his duffel bag. Three vodka nips were left where they were, but he decided to take the other two with him, as well as his phone. At that point he decided to extract a little of the white powder from the five gram packet. He ripped a piece of plastic from a shopping bag and dumped what looked to his eyes to be a little more than a gram onto it. To close it he used the metal twist tie from the bag of "biscotti cantucci" that Maurizio had bought in the local specialties store. He put the gram and a half in his pocket. The rest he hid in the drawer of the bedside table between some underwear and a pair of socks. With the duffel bag on his shoulder, he got into his car and headed towards Giulia's house.

When he reached Corbara ten minutes later, the reporter was leaving, headed in the direction of Ascoli Piceno.

Since there wasn't any cellphone signal he couldn't call her, so he decided to follow her.

PART THREE

Ascoli Piceno
Piazza del Popolo
Wednesday June 20, 20XX
8:43 PM

The city of a hundred towers. The city of travertine. The city full of churches. The city of St. Emidio. The city of Cecco d'Ascoli. The city of the Quintana festival. The city of fried olives. The city of beautiful women. The city of the ancient Piceni, who defeated the ancient Romans. The city of soccer icon Costantino Rozzi. The city of Carnevale. The city of...

While wandering around Ascoli, Maurizio had come to appreciate how much the Ascolani loved their city.

His plan had been to take a break in the provincial capital all by himself, and he had done well. In this very moment he was enjoying a serene solitude. Solitude that, all day long, he had alternated with casual company; a pair of baristas, a news vendor, a waiter, three drinking companions met in three different bars, another diner alone like he was at a table in a restaurant he'd chosen for its strange sign — CaSomai — and finally, a clerk in a bookstore in the town center.

In addition, he had discovered that, while there was certainly fear regarding the earthquake tremors — which since that morning had menaced the whole zone — the citizens of Ascoli enjoyed the protection of St.Emidio, patron saint of the city and protector from earthquakes (not of earthquakes as someone had told him). And this, even if he wasn't a believer, had provided him with a further sense of positivity.

The miracle of optimism.

Unjustified optimism, but so what?

He had done his duty towards resolving his house problem. He had even taken on a lawyer.

And not only that.

Breathing the clean air of this small provincial town had helped him to distance himself from the oppressive sensation he'd felt in Montegallo, and yet remain loyal to the idea of staying far from the big city.

It's true he wasn't completely relaxed. The much loved house in the mountains had brought nothing but stress, but hope — they say — is the last thing to die.

He hoped that the next day would be different.

Soon he would choose a restaurant for dinner. It had been such a positive day, why not enjoy it up to the end?

The only off note: the lawyer Bonanni.

He hadn't liked him at all, but he had to trust him. Even the casual acquaintances he'd made that day had confirmed that Bonanni was the best.

There was a second off note as he got into his car.

Another earthquake tremor.

Via Salaria
Direction Ascoli Piceno
Tony Liberati's Car
Wednesday June 20, 20XX
9:04 PM

Giulia sat in the passenger seat next to Tony, talking. She told an exciting story rich in details, very straightforward.

Tony was agitated. As he moved his feet over the clutch, accelerator and brake in a dance at the edge of control, he himself was at the edge of control.

He had caught up with the journalist about ten kilometers from Ascoli. By flashing his headlights and blasting his horn, he had succeeded in attracting her attention. Giulia had pulled her car over and gotten into his with her precious laptop, leaving him with his mouth agape.

He, who had imagined he would have to present himself full of apologies and with a declaration of intentions based on civil comportment, common sense, blah, blah, blah, found himself called to play the part of the friend you could ask for help. Trusted friend, the only one. At that moment, indispensible.

Who else could Giulia have turned to? Nobody. Nobody else would believe her. She had just called Dr. Antonini and he had told her that everything was in order at the Forte Malatesta and that the work had been completed in the agreed upon time. He had also confirmed that the fortress would be inaugurated on Saturday the 23rd with the opening of the exhibit that at present was still in the process of being mounted.

But Giulia wouldn't give up. Convinced that her friend was a prisoner in a cell within the ancient fortress, and that she had asked for help in a dream, she had decided to get to the bottom of it.

Logical, no?

Signora Cantarini found in the lunatic Liberati a knight ready to show his valor in something which she announced in advance would be a veritable commando raid.

"The fort is set in a defensive position on the left bank of the Castellano River," she said, describing the place they were headed towards. "In the pre-Roman and Roman eras there was a bulwark which blocked access to the bridge."

She'd started to show him the photos on her laptop.

Tony darted quick glances in between vigorous shifts into higher gears, gripping the gearshaft with virile determination.

"It was destroyed and rebuilt several times. In 1349 Galeotto Malatesta, condottiero of the Ascolani troops in the war against Fermo, reinforced it and made it into a typical medieval fort."

He listened without asking any questions, but he couldn't absorb it all. By now Giulia was going full steam ahead.

"More destruction followed until, in the beginning of the 1500's, a twelve-sided church dedicated to Santa Maria del Lago was constructed in the ruins of the fortress. Although deconsecrated it still exists within the central body of the present edifice."

A thought came into his brain. He figured he better put it out there right away, to spotlight the close attention ... with which he was following things ... that he remembered every detail. "Another church named for the Madonna ... and water again ... there's a lake involved in this?"

"Bravo. In fact a Roman era thermal spa was the first structure built on the site in question. But let me finish, listen to me ... and take the next exit ... Okay, where was I?"

"At the twelve-sided church."

They entered a tunnel.

"In 1543 Antonio da San Gallo the Younger erected a new fort in the shape of an irregular star on this same site. In 1878 the fort was renovated and it was used as a judicial prison until 1978." Showing him another photo, she concluded, "This is what it looks like today."

"And this?"

"The Ponte di Cecco — Cecco's Bridge — that little stone structure houses the gateway to the city. The bridge was definitely of Roman construction from the Republican era. Even when the original was destroyed during World War II it was reconstructed exactly the way it was. Popular tradition says it was built by the Devil in a single night, on the orders of Cecco D'Ascoli, local alchemist and astrologer."

At Giulia's direction, Tony parked the car behind a restaurant. Strategically situated at one end of the Ponte Maggiore, the bridge that led to the eastern door of the old city, at one time this building had been the ancient customs house.

Large raindrops began to splatter on the windshield. Hesitating in the last moments of indecision, the two observed the gloomy shape of the fortress silhouetted in the darkness before their eyes.

Giulia took the initiative. "Okay, let's go!"

"Wait."

"Have you changed your mind? All right, I'll go by myself."

"What are you saying?" Tony was searching for something under his seat.

"What are you doing?"

"Here they are! These might be helpful." He pulled out two nine-caliber Beretta pistols and a box of bullets.

"You're crazy!"

Giulia opened the door and started to get out, but Tony grabbed her arm.

"No, listen, they aren't real. They're like real ones, but they don't shoot . . . that is, they shoot, but they only make noise. They're safe, theater props, the same as real ones but harmless. But the effect is very convincing."

While talking he showed her the clip, which he loaded with blanks.

"I don't want one. Take them if you think it's necessary, but not for me."

"As you wish."

He pulled his shirt out of his pants and stuck the pistols through the belt of his jeans.

He got out of the car.

The rain was falling violently.

They started to run towards the barred gates.

Lightning split the sky, illuminating for an instant the spectral profile of the Forte Malatesta.

Ascoli Piceno
Forte Malatesta
Wednesday June 20, 20XX
9:27 PM

A thunderstorm worthy of the most terrifying horror film hurled an impressive amount of water onto the city. The epicenter of the precipitation seemed to be the Forte Malatesta.

Locked metal gates halted Giulia and Tony's initial approach.

The last time she had been here — the journalist remembered it well — the reconstruction worksite occupied all the surrounding area. Scaffolding, machinery, and workers crowded everywhere.

Momentarily immobilized, undecided about what to do, drenched by the pounding rain, they stared at the edifice and its windows in search of a sign, an idea.

The Castellano River rumbled furiously under the Ponte Maggiore, the lightening threw violent flashes on the rain-swollen clouds.

"Come on, we'll go this way," Giulia said.

She turned back and then took a left towards a large gate. This one too looked barred, but a light push opened it; it was unlatched. Passing through the gate they found themselves on the perimeter road that ran along the south side of the fortress, heading for the riverbank. The roar of the raging water was ever nearer, ever more violent. They crossed in front of the Ponte Cecco and ascended a ramp of stone steps, ending up on the other side of the iron bars that had impeded their path.

Great. Now they had to find a way to get into the building.

They opted for the simplest solution. Approaching the main door, the one the guests at the imminent inauguration would enter, Giulia buzzed the intercom.

"And you think someone's going to open it? Gimme a break!"

"Come on, what do we have to lose?"

"Oh, nothing. If there are bad guys inside now they know there's an intruder at the door. They could come out and kidnap us too, or they could kill us by shooting out a window, or..."

The lock rattled.

Tony stepped to one side, with his back against the wall. He pulled out one of the two pistols and indicated to his accomplice that she should stand in front of the door, then he muttered under his breath, "Damn, just like I've always dreamed!"

Giulia had no time to object. The door opened.

A beautiful dark haired girl appeared.

Perhaps a hostess working to organize the event scheduled for Saturday.

Impassive and elegant in her blue outfit, the shadow that passed over her face at the sight of an unknown person was the only flaw in an otherwise perfect imperturbability. This was not one of the expected guests; although surprised, the girl did not lost control. With extreme politeness, she greeted the woman. "Good evening. In what way may I help you?"

"Good evening. Uhhh...my car broke down right at the end of the bridge, and since...ahh...I don't have my cellphone with me, I need..."

Not too believable as lies go, could have done better. To make up for it she gestured, pointing at the parking lot. By retreating half a pace she lured the girl into coming outside.

The girl took two steps forward.

Tony pointed the pistol at her temple.

"Okay, stay calm. Don't make a move and nothing will happen to you."

"What are you doing?"

Tony Liberati, the hero... scornful of any danger, he opened a path through his enemies. Great film, great action, great role.

Giulia was dumbfounded.

"Leave this to me. Put your hands behind your head! Go back in and lead the way."

"Tony, don't overdo it. She could be a city employee."

A little too calm to just be an employee. The reporter thought it over. No, this one was definitely something other than an employee. Okay then. She would back up Tony. They would go ahead with this absurd game, which after all, she herself had started.

"All right, but I'll go first. I know where to look. I toured the fortress from top to bottom when I came here to write that article. The cell is down there, it's the only one that has a stone with a sun carved on it."

She went ahead. Behind her, in single file, the lovely brunette — hands clasped behind her neck — and Tony, with the barrel of the nine-caliber in his fist, continuously repeating to the girl to be quiet. A jammed CD would have been less annoying.

The girl tried to raise an objection, but she wasn't allowed to. Tony immediately signaled to keep her mouth shut.

The inside of the Forte Malatesta looked to be in fine condition. The restoration had kept the original peculiarities, starting with the division of the space. Stone and wood were the prevalent building materials.

Suddenly Tony had the sensation of hearing a buzz, a babble of voices from deep down, but he didn't say anything. Giulia knew what to do and where to look.

She headed straight for a corridor marked with a sign, "Section 1." After following it for about fifteen meters, she stopped in front of a heavy wooden door painted grey. Her frantic shove opened it, squeaking.

There was nobody inside.

In the center of the ceiling was the stone sculpted with the radiating symbols of Jesus that she had recognized in her dream. No trace of Morgana. Actually, there were traces—a cot with rumpled sheets, a bowl with the remains of boiled rice and a half full bottle of water—but nothing that proved that it was Signora Bucci who had been here. She tried a bluff.

"Listen to me closely; tell me where we can find the woman you were holding prisoner in this place. Tell me now, otherwise my friend will make a hole in your head, and goodbye to your pretty little face."

Tony, true to the part that this extraordinary script has assigned him, pulled the slide back, loading a cartridge into the chamber, then cocked the hammer with the most theatrical gesture possible.

The girl replied instantly without any sign of fear. "She is undergoing the purification ritual in preparation for tomorrow."

"Where? Where is she now?"

"Right above us. On the top floor of the church of Santa Maria del Lago."

"Let's go. I know where that is."

"So long, sweetie. By the way, I would never have shot you, and anyway it's a fake. I'm for making love, not war."

"Let's go, hurry!"

They bolted the heavy door, leaving their fair guide a prisoner.

"Follow me." After looking around for a few seconds, she chose the passageway that would lead to the highest floor of the fort.

Ascoli Piceno
Forte Malatesta
Wednesday June 20. 20XX
9:48 PM

Stairs, stairs and more stairs.

Giulia knew they had to reach the highest of the three levels contained within the lofty twelve-sided building, at one time the church of Santa Maria del Lago.

Finally they arrived at a doorway. From behind the heavy red curtain that protected the entrance came the sound of a chorus chanting. The words were incomprehensible.

She took a peek, moving aside the edge of the fabric where a little light filtered through. "I see people dressed in white. With their faces covered by white hoods."

"How many are there?"

"I don't know. I can only see small sections of the room. It's really big, the voices seem to come from every side. Wait, I see Morgana! It's Morgana!"

"Shh, shh, talk more quietly. They might hear you."

"She's standing in the center of the room. Dressed in a white tunic. Now they're making her bend down over a big container, full of water, I think. A hooded guy is filling a pitcher and pouring it on her head."

"Okay, all right. They're baptizing her. But what film are you watching?'

"If you don't believe me, look for yourself."

Tony took the journalist's place. "You're right! Now he's got a big candle and he's making signs in the air with the flame right in front of Morgana's eyes."

"Let me see."

Giulia reclaimed the peephole, so Tony took a look around. He went over to a window, running his hands through his hair. "Damn, how high up are we?"

The reporter answered without removing her eyes from the figure who was sprinkling a fistful of dirt on Morgana's head. "We're a couple hundred feet above the river."

Tony stopped looking outside and started rummaging through his pockets. "Okay, that's enough of playing detectives. Now we're calling the Carabinieri."

A few seconds was all it took for his expression to mutate from incredulity to suspicion to something bordering on fear.

"I left my cellphone in the car, when I was sticking the pistols in my belt. It was in the way, it was bothering me . . . so I set it on the back seat. Shit!"

"Don't worry, I've got . . ." Giulia tried to reassure him. She started looking for her cellphone. But the more she searched, the more her face recapitulated the gallery of shadings put on display by Tony a few moments earlier.

"Nooo! I left mine in the car too! In my car! I plugged it into the charger after I talked to Antonini, since I'd been using it continuously. I was afraid it would run out of juice during an emergency."

"Exactly."

More anxious than ever about her friend's situation, she went back to spying. In the center of the room, she saw another hooded figure rise up; in his hand was a knife with an ivory handle.

Terror took possession of her. The glittering blade was passed through the flame, into the water, and then directed towards Morgana's face, but served only to moisten the dirt in her hair. Giulia let out a big sigh of relief before she spoke. "We have to do something. Give me the pistol."

"And then?"

"We'll go in there and free Morgana."

"What the hell are you saying? It's full of fanatics in there. Maybe one of them is armed too."

"I knew it. You're a classic Roman blowhard. I'll go by myself."

"I'll show you who's the blowhard..."

Going over to the window sill, he put his hand in his pocket and brought forth the little packet of cocaine. With a twenty euro banknote he prepared a copious line of white powder.

Giulia watched him with contempt and then went back to the peephole. And Morgana, where was she?

She pricked up her ears trying to understand the words pronounced inside the room, but the only thing she could hear clearly was the prolonged snorting of Tony's nostril.

"Now, let's make our entrance!" The actor said when he finished. He took the extra pistol and after he had loaded a slug in the chamber, he gave it to Giulia. Finally, he showed her how to release the safety.

"Let's go. Do what I tell you."

Pushing aside the curtain with his left arm, he took two steps forward and, holding the pistol horizontally, he burst into the cavernous hall.

"Okay, people, stay calm! There's been a change of plans."

Giulia followed him, also with a pistol in her hand. Each of them had half the room covered — so to speak.

After a few moments of confusion, a small band of hooded figures advanced menacingly. Tony fired twice into the air.

Nobody took notice of the fact that there were no bullet holes in the ceiling. Confused by the echo of the shots, the assembly seemed intimidated by the sudden incursion.

"Come on, Morgana, let's go. We're out of here!" Giulia turned to her friend, who didn't need to be asked twice. Without saying a word she took refuge between her saviors.

"Don't you think you're a little outnumbered?" It was the Grand Master who spoke. "Probably you haven't taken into account where you are. Probably you haven't the slightest idea of what it is that you have interrupted."

He moved forward with slow steps, giving the armed couple the time and opportunity to notice the six-pointed stars inlaid in the pavement, the points corresponding to six of the twelve corners of the room.

By now a group of the adepts had placed themselves in front of the door. Motionless, they surrounded the odd trio.

"Your friend runs no risk. Her life is precious, a gift of grace for our Brotherhood. We are ready to receive the divine vision generated by the power of the one who has been sent at the hour of the union of the great father Sun and the great mother Moon."

"Liar! It's true you want me alive, but only until tomorrow, until the summer solstice! You're a common murderer!" Morgana screamed at her jailer with all the rage accumulated during those desperate hours in which she had been forced to maintain, as much as possible, a certain level of lucidity and coolness. "And now, enough with this charade! Augusto, take off that ridiculous hood. I'm only ashamed that I didn't understand sooner what a foul being I was dealing with."

"But what...?" Giulia didn't have time to finish her sentence before the Count Piloni de Castris took off his disguise revealing to all his true face.

"I always thought you were a total asshole."

Without taking notice of Tony's remark, the Count spoke to those present: "Now it is no longer necessary to maintain any further reserve. From tomorrow I will be — and you with me — the depository of an infinite power, the power of knowledge. Knowledge of the future, which signifies total control of events, starting with those economic and political. Absolute manipulation of the human species..."

"But this guy is mad as a hatter!"

Giulia took her friend by the arm and with a glance urged Tony to leave. He moved towards the exit, then had a second thought. Retracing his steps, he went up to the Count: "I repeat: I always thought you were a total asshole."

"I believe you and, so as not to disappoint your expectations, dear sir, I would like to announce to all present that the weapons of the lady and gentleman are fakes. One can see that clearly from the shape of the cartridge clips. They are too narrow to hold real bullets, they're just blanks."

Ascoli Piceno
Forte Malatesta
Wednesday June 20, 20XX
10:14 PM

The words pronounced by the Grand Master reinvigorated the disciples and threw the two intruders into disarray. Even more dismayed was the designated victim.

The band that earlier had been on the point of intervening now encircled them.

Pointing their guns in every direction, Tony and Giulia realized that they had no other choice but to carry out their bluff to the last degree.

They fired into the air.

And this time the devotees looked up.

No holes, not even a scratch.

The knot of attendants closed around them. They were captured and carried before the Count for further instructions.

Giulia kept on bluffing. "Don't do anything stupid. Before we broke in we telephoned the Carabinieri, who must be about to arrive, or maybe they're already here. Let us go."

Some went to peer out the windows, but nobody thought to search the intruders for their cellphones.

Turning to the group of fanatics who were restraining them, the Count said, "Lock those two in a cell, and we'll leave. We can't risk missing tomorrow's appointment. Go on, hurry."

"Why don't we kill them?" someone suggested.

"That could create more problems than it solves. I don't think anybody will believe their story, they will sound too crazy, and we will have all the time we need. Everybody leave by the secret passageway; after that you know what to do. We'll see each other tomorrow at the appointed place and time." Then, turning to the two figures who held Morgana, "Bring her with us."

Everybody left, last of all the gang who had immobilized the prisoners by twisting their arms behind their backs.

This time they didn't go up or down any stairs, they were simply locked in a room situated on the same floor as the deconsecrated church. Unlike where Morgana had been imprisoned, this was not a cell. No bed, no table, no chairs; only packing crates and a big unbarred window.

"Now what are we going to do?" It was Tony who spoke, while Giulia paced back and forth.

"We have to get out of here as quickly as possible. We have to inform the Carabinieri or the police."

"Yes, but how?"

"We have until tomorrow, then they'll kill her."

"True. We have to think." He sat down on a box. "How do we get out of here before tomorrow morning? There's always the hope that someone will show up for work in this shithole."

Giulia didn't stop walking and talking.

"Count Augusto Piloni de Castris! I can't believe it, he's completely crazy. We have to stop him."

"Okay, but stay calm," Tony suggested, followed by a nasal snort that left no doubt about how little calmness had to do with his state of mind.

"Do you want to leave her in the lurch so you can get high?"

"Huh! Get high! That's an exaggeration. And anyway if I get out of here alive, tomorrow I'm quitting. I swear."

"That's what everybody says. But look at who I've had to..."

"Hey, check this out!" He had started to rummage in a half opened box. Inside were various objects destined for display in the exhibit currently being mounted. "We can try to unhinge the door with this."

He meant Leonardo Da Vinci's jack. It was wooden but functioned perfectly. To improve his cultural education, and to pick up some useful hints, he set himself to reading the plastic card that explained the jack's history and use. Then he got to work, first maneuvering the contraption over against the door.

"This is useless." After a series of attempts that pushed the limits of the absurd, he eventually had to give up. "I can't wedge it underneath."

Skeptical, and disgusted by the pathetic spectacle offered by her companion in misfortune, Giulia dedicated herself to exploring another box. Her lingering mistrust didn't give her much hope, but she concentrated intensely on reading another plastic card.

Then she moved over to a window to look down at a point far below, in the dark.

A few minutes of engrossed contemplation and she returned to the crate. She began to apply herself to the assembly of a pyramidal contraption, a wooden structure with a square base to which were attached four panels of heavy fabric that met together in a single point. Ropes dangled from a central point inside the vertex of the pyramid.

After that she clutched a big plank that had been part of the packing and hit the double glass of the window. One, two, three times. Nothing happened.

Shatterproof glass.

She turned to Tony. "Come here, give me a hand."

Together, giving it all they had, they succeeded in breaking the window.

"But what do you want to do? Yell? Great. Look where we are, on the side over the river. Oh shit, that's a long way down!"

Giulia didn't answer. She grabbed the cloth pyramid. "Come on, help me. Don't just stand there admiring the view."

"You want to throw that thing down there? What for?"

"I'm not going to throw it. I just wanted to see if it'll make it through the window, and as you can see, it fits just fine."

"And then what?"

"Read this."

The plastic card.

Fixated on understanding the words printed on the card, he found himself caught in a tangle of rope. With dawning comprehension and incredulity regarding Giulia's plan, he didn't have much strength to resist. "But you're crazy! This is a reproduction . . . Okay, do you understand? Re-pro-duc-tion of a parachute designed in the 1500's. In the fif-teen-hun-dreds! And you want me to throw myself into space in this thingamajig?

"Why not? It's a reproduction, but a faithful one. And as far as the date goes, what's the problem? Leonardo wasn't Leonardo by accident. Anyway, calm down. I'm not going to abandon you, I'll be holding on. We'll jump together, in a big hug!"

"You don't know what you're saying."

"Listen to me: it'll work. Plus we don't have any alternative. They're going to kill Morgana if we don't find them in time."

"But what film are you in, 007? For your information my name is Tony. Tony Liberati, not James Bond. Not even Indiana Jones. At least he had a boat. Another crazy . . ."

Saying that, he pulled out what remained of his stock of cocaine. He tipped it out on the window sill in a single line — a thick line — but right when he was about to give himself up to the pleasure of a healthy snort, Giulia took him by surprise.

"Okay that's enough! That shit is over!"

The journalist blew on the line. Nothing remained of the precious powder.

"What the hell are you doing? You're crazy! How dare you . . . you know what I say to you? Go take a jump by yourself."

"Fine. Give me that."

She grabbed his arm to loosen up the ropes, screaming her distain into her dazed companion's face. "You know how ridiculous you are? You're hiding behind the presumed suffering of the artist which is nothing more than ineptitude. The pure incapacity to live. You're a loser, that's what you are!"

"Shut up! Be quiet! And stop messing around with stuff. Let's go. Take this rope and climb on my back. From now until we land I don't want to hear anything more out of you!"

Signora Cantarini didn't have the strength to fight back. She was tired and scared to death, but at this point she couldn't quit. She clutched onto the back of the only possibility of salvation that was left to her. A remote possibility, given the circumstances and the hero's lack of balls. And she was entrusting her life to him?

Straining his leg muscles because of the extra weight, Tony climbed up onto the windowsill.

Once he had set his feet on the surface, he concentrated on the prototype of a parachute. Pulling on the ropes, he was able to drag the contraption close to them. He and Giulia grabbed onto it and positioned it over their heads, supporting it with their hands.

They looked out. The lights of the apartment buildings that rose up on the opposite bank of the Castellano River glittered in the distance, the only sign of human life in the pitch darkness. The torrent roared impetuously below them. Many meters below. The cold rain whipped their cheeks and eyes without pity, making every reference point confused and surreal.

Giulia held tight, her hands clasped high on Tony's chest.

They launched themselves into the void.

Screaming.

A sudden sharp jerk silenced them.

Then the sensation of being suspended in the night.

A lightning bolt flashed in the sky.

For an instant they could make out the trees, the rocks, and the water fast approaching.

The impact!

The dark.

Ascoli Piceno
Ponte Maggiore
Wednesday June 20,20XX
10:48 PM

Despite the thunderstorm, Maurizio drove serenely, listening to one of his favorite CDs. Like all of his CDs, it was a compilation he had put together himself.

The song — "In un Giorno di Pioggia" — was by the Modena City Ramblers.

He was making his way towards the Via Salaria, and then to the cutoff after Mozzano that would carry him to Montegallo. Leaving the city center traveling east, he crossed the Ponte Maggiore, the bridge with the same name as the gate by which it entered the city. Lightning lit up the sky over the ancient medieval fortress, which someone had told him would be open to visitors in a few days.

A dart of light that tore through the clouds to his right attracted his attention.

What he saw in that instant, lasting as long as a photographer's flashbulb, seemed incredible, the fruit of a hallucination.

A window on the top floor of the Forte Malatesta had spit out a sort of white dome from which was suspended a human outline.

He pulled the car over to the edge of the sidewalk that ran along the parapet and got out.

Advancing along the bridge he kept his eyes on the area where he thought he'd glimpsed that apparition.

Pitch dark. Impossible to see anything. Another lightning bolt blazed.

There it was, the body. No, the bodies!

Hanging from a rudimentary parachute.

He heard a scream.

He saw them falling past the little bridge arched in the background, the Ponte di Cecco he seemed to recall. They disappeared into the deafening sound of the rushing waters.

Ascoli Piceno
Mazzoni Hospital
Emergency Room
Thursday June 21, 20XX
2:57 AM

Side by side, waiting to be taken to their respective wards, Tony and Giulia couldn't stop talking about their adventure.

In the emergency room of Ascoli Piceno's hospital, in the area reserved for patients under observation, Marshal Moser and Maurizio Verdimani listened to the incredible tale told by the injured parties. Having received initial treatment, but not yet assigned hospital beds, the two competed in interrupting, talking over, and then in backing up each other's story.

A story of occult rituals — human sacrifices — of a hostage in danger — Morgana — of a mysterious sect — a group of hooded figures — and a crazy high priest — the esteemed Count Augusto Piloni de Castris himself.

The two survivors didn't seem to have suffered too much damage, but to take every precaution the doctors had decided to hospitalize them for further assessment.

Luckily, Maurizio had called for help right away.

An ambulance had arrived in a few minutes. The firemen had retrieved the imitators of Icarus, who had ended up on the rocks near the banks of the Castellano River.

Both had hit their heads, but only Tony had lost consciousness; both had scrapes and scratches, but only Tony needed stitches; both had bruised bones, but only Tony had two broken ribs; both were extremely worried about Morgana's safety, but only Tony had asked for a double vodka on the rocks.

He was not granted this satisfaction. On the contrary it was Giulia who was satisfied, because Marshal Moser had believed her. Her version had seemed more logical and circumstantiated than the actor's even though, in reality, they had said fundamentally the same things.

Giulia had implored the officer to do whatever he could to find her friend as soon as possible. He gave orders to start the search right away.

"The provincial command isn't holding back any manpower," he stated, "We have only one problem, in the Montemonaco area, where a museum theft was reported an hour ago. Our first priority is to figure out the location of the appointed place to which the Count referred, so that we can concentrate our forces."

"But I beg you! They talked about the summer solstice. Morgana said that she would be kept alive up until that moment. If I'm not mistaken, the solstice occurs at an exact time."

"True. The solstice is set for today at 12:26, we've already ascertained that."

Maurizio listened in silence. Every so often he glanced at Tony, who continued to snort and sniffle.

"Did they do any blood tests?" he asked his friend.

"Of course, the usual tests, nothing special."

Ascoli Piceno
Mazzoni Hospital
Women's Medical Ward
Thursday June 21, 20XX
6:57 AM

Sleep was not an option. Around four in the morning Giulia had turned on her laptop and she was still there, connected to the internet, looking for reports of any possible esoteric ritual that had to do with the summer solstice. She was 100% sure of one thing: the day and the hour. In the year 20XX the summer solstice would occur on June 21 at exactly 12:26 PM.

What she didn't know was where the Brotherhood would gather to celebrate the bloody rite. A very precise spot—already agreed upon, according to the Count—but which?

The experts of the Carabinieri were pursuing this, but nevertheless she wasn't able to relax, and not just because she was worried about Morgana's fate. Another problem buzzed in her head keeping her awake. A quite stimulating problem.

Her book.

How depressing to be stuck in this bed, feeling passive, helpless, unable to keep up with events. She had been right in the thick of things until now. She didn't want to run the risk of being left behind just when the story had taken a truly disturbing turn for the worse.

Really, she should have been happy not to have suffered any serious damage after a flight of more than 200 feet embracing a man suspended from a 16th century parachute.

Happy that it was only an intravenous tube that tied her to this bed.

And, after all, there was something she could do here — in this bed.

The Carabinieri, at her request, had delivered her computer and personal effects, which they'd recovered from her car parked alongside the road.

She had telephoned her newspaper and alerted them that the next day she would have an extraordinary piece, for which they should reserve sufficient space.

Too bad though, that despite all her online research, she couldn't find anything illuminating in the traditions of the Piceno backcountry relative to possible superstitions or to ancient pagan rites concerning this precise day of the year.

To distract herself she opened the newspapers a nice nurse had brought her when the shifts changed.

She turned immediately to the regional news, where the big story was the earthquake. In the local column the phrase "seismic zone" was most prominent.

An article of a few lines and on a totally different subject suddenly grabbed her attention.

Thursday June 21, 20XX

CORRIERE ADRIATICO

MYSTERIOUS THEFT AT MONTEMONACO
THE "GREAT STONE" STOLEN FROM THE MUSEUM OF THE SIBYL

The "Great Stone" was stolen Tuesday night in Montemonaco by unknown persons. The theft has been verified by the Museum of the Sibyl, which is dedicated to the cave of legendary fairy enchantress, considered the oracle *par excellence* of the pagan world. The missing object is a flat rock originally found on the spit of land that divides the twin basins of the Lago di Pilato. In remote times, the Lago di Pilato was the chosen destination of sorcerers, wizards, and magicians, who performed blasphemous rites on this particular narrow strip of earth.

The stone is marked by rudimentary carvings, mysterious letters that are still the subject of study. Scholars suggest that it could be a sacrificial altar, or a stele on which demonic invocations have been incised.

There seems to be no mystery however regarding the motive which would have led the thief or thieves to steal only the "Great Stone." The Carabinieri involved in the investigation are certain that they are dealing with a theft done on commission, given the uniqueness of the piece. Without doubt, it is the most precious object in the small museum.

A simple association of ideas came into Giulia's mind: lake, Sibyl, sacrificial altar, sorcerers plus water, female divinity, Morgana, the Count Piloni de Castris.

The location of the Lago di Pilato fit perfectly all the characteristics that, up until that moment, had distinguished the Sibillini crimes. Although it wasn't a cult site dedicated to the Madonna, it still represented a place of great significance in the veneration of the Sibyl, one of the highest female divinities in the pagan world.

During the research she had done at Morgana's house, she remembered reading that the oldest testimony relative to the cult of the Sibyl dated to the 1300's, in the works of Pietro Bersuire and Fazio degli Uberti. Situated near the Sibyl's cave, the Lago di Pilato was referred to as the spot where books of magic were consecrated, where evoked spirits obeyed whoever gave them his own soul in exchange. This motif reappeared through the successive centuries in accounts of direct experiences and in popular legends.

Going online, Giulia tracked down various historic documents that contained references to the Lago di Pilato: Flavio Biondo, Enea Silvio Piccolomini (the future Pope Pio I), Fra Bernardino Bonavoglia, Pietro Antonio Caracciolo, Luigi Pulci, Giovanni delle Piatte, Nicolò Pieranzoni, Leandro degli Alberti, Ludovico Ariosto, Benvenuto Cellini...

The lake's reknown had been seen and framed in the context of the concepts and beliefs of the epoch. It was a time in which they believed in sorcerers, and wrote works on the search for treasures and on the methods for calling up spirits. It was the time of John of Salisbury, of Ugo di S. Vittore, of Cecco d'Ascoli, of Gerolamo Cardano and of other eminent devotees of magic; a world of visionaries according to whom human happiness had to take into consideration the pursuit of self-interest, the realization of ambitions, the search for sensuality; a world that wanted to overcome at any cost the divide between reality and the recurring dreams of spells and occult practices, in such a way as to put the supernatural forces at the disposition of impotent mankind.

But why was the Lago di Pilato held in such high regard by these devotees of magic?

According to Peranzoni (1510), it was due to the solitude of the place, and to the characters incised on the stones, work of Cecco d'Ascoli and of Virgil, essential for the exercise of magical practices.

The reference to the "Great Stone" was clear.

According to Alberti and Magini, concerning the agitation of the waters, "With perpetual movements they rise and fall to the great wonder of those who gaze upon them, up here where the credulous people believe that the demons live and if called upon, will respond."

For the people, in fact, the lake was cursed.

And the people, needing an explanation, had turned to fantasy. They had created a legend surrounding a character of inauspicious repute, as inauspicious as the repute of a solitary place, of an inscribed stone, of a lake's surface agitated by obscure currents.

Pontius Pilate.

Who could be more accursed than him?

Historically Pilate had no connection with the Sibillini, but the people, of course, didn't really care about history.

According to the people, his accursed corpse had been carried to the top of the mountain by wild oxen and dumped with a mighty noise into the waters of the lake.

Not coincidentally, the legend of Pilate was one of those most worked over by popular fantasy.

Not coincidentally, there were various locations which laid claim to his mortal remains, and all of them frightening and threatening in the same way. A swamp near Losanna, the Lago Nero in the Valley of Corvegno, a cursed mountain near Lucerne, and finally Monte Vettore with its lake.

Giulia was convinced.

The theft of the stone was connected to the Count's sect and to the sacrifice of Morgana: her friend would be killed at 12:26 on the spit of land in the middle of the Lago di Pilato.

She was so sure of it that she phoned Moser right away. After listening to her excited deductions the marshal threw cold water on them. "No, no, don't worry. Our experts have already determined the place that de Castris was referring to."

"But..."

"Basically it's still thanks to you, since all we did was follow the theory of the constellation of the Virgin, which you had pointed out to us."

"But are you sure? Because..."

"We have no doubts. We're concentrating all our men on the area of the Santuario of the Madonna dell'Ambro, the most significant site on the map of the churches named after the Holy Virgin."

In fact, it was one of the churches described in Professor Roiati's book, and it was also the most important sanctuary in the zone, built moreover close to a course of water, the Ambro brook. But it still wasn't the right place.

"Marshal, you're wrong. Listen to me, I beg you..."

"I have to go now, but don't worry. I'll keep you informed."

Montegallo
Village of Astorara
Maurizio Verdimani's House
Thursday June 21, 20XX
8:22PM

As opposed to the day that had preceded it, the night had been just terrible for Maurizio.

Nothing compared to what Tony and Giulia had presumably experienced, but the fear and stress accumulated in these last hours had deprived him of the restorative sleep he'd been looking forward to during his return trip from the hospital.

The vision of his friends lying motionless on the rocky river bank, their bloody faces glimpsed in the dark and to all appearances lifeless, the frenzied arrival of the emergency vehicles, the feverish recovery of the bodies by the firemen, then the unexpected news of the good condition of the wounded...

His agitated half-sleep was interrupted by the cellphone.

"Hello..."

"Hi, it's me. Listen..."

"Hello..."

"Mauri, it's Giulia! Listen, you have to go up to Monte Vettore to the Lago di Pilato..."

Terrible night.

The day would be even worse.

He had a hard time believing his own ears, listening without understanding as words and phrases poured forth in an unstoppable stream. Several times he tried to fight back, but to every reasonable objection the reporter responded with an irrefutable reproach: the danger that Morgana was running, the obtuse indifference of the Carabinieri who were convinced that they would find the sect convened at the Santuario dell'Ambro, the impossibility — for her, confined to bed — to cover in person the most important story of her life.

There was nothing to do but make promises. He would leave immediately. He would reach the Lago di Pilato in time to save Morgana's life.

But how?

Anselmo Grossi.

He would ask his friend for help. His friend the wood-cutter, ex-Alpine Military Force and mountain territory expert; who could be a better guide?

By 9 AM he was already in the passenger seat of Grossi's pick-up truck heading for Foce di Montemonaco.

The trail to the Lago di Pilato starts there.

Ascoli Piceno
Mazzoni Hospital
Men's Orthopedic Ward
Thursday June 21, 20XX
10:51 AM

The drugs which had allowed him to rest for some hours without suffering from the pain of his two broken ribs were wearing off. Now that he was reemerging bit by bit from the anesthetic fog, he had to find a way to deal with the discomfort.

He decided to not think about it.

Tony had never been able to stand pain, but at the same time, he had discovered that you could distract yourself. Many times he had experienced how the power of the mind acted on the body with undeniable efficacy. Nothing to do with meditation techniques or other new age practices, which were very far from his philosophy of life, what he needed was a material distraction, given that the thought process is in itself a concrete action.

He had to find something to do, something to think about, something to chew on.

Before leaving, Maurizio had delivered his cellphone and duffel bag to his room. In the outer pocket of the last he remembered he had placed the flashdrive and the two discs that Angelo Di Pietro had given him.

The only thing lacking was a laptop.

Giulia! Of course! He hadn't yet told her the story of the bribes paid by Forlan to the mayor of Montegallo.

He asked a nurse about the journalist's condition. The entire hospital was talking about the adventure in which he'd been a protagonist, so the head of the ward was very willing to take a message to the other celebrity of the moment, currently in the women's section of the hospital.

Shortly thereafter, Signora Cantarini presented herself at the bedside of her companion in misfortune, eager to confide her suspicions to him.

It was she, however, who was astounded by Tony's revelations. First he summarized the gist of the information he'd gotten from Senator Cecchini, then he asked to borrow her laptop so he could replay the video of the conversation with His Honor.

Giulia didn't hesitate for a second. More material at her disposal, and what material! Hot stuff to say the least!

Tony took over her computer to look at the contents of the flashdrive and disks.

The reporter immersed herself in listening to the intimate confessions of the scantily dressed politician.

Montemonaco
Foce — Trail to the Lago di Pilato
Thursday June 21, 20XX
11:33 AM

They had just passed, on the left, the ruins of a cabin. Capanna Piscini, according to Anselmo, who kept talking so as to distract Maurizio from his exhaustion. Unlike the wood cutter, the archivist was not used to an environment as difficult and inaccessabile as these mountains, nor to the remarkable effort they were exerting in order to arrive at the Lago di Pilato in time.

More than remarkable. Superhuman.

There wasn't much time left til 12:26, the hour at which — according to Giulia — Count Augusto would kill Morgana, sacrificing her to who knows what divinity.

The most difficult stretch was the rocky switchback called "delle Svolte" — "The Curves."

The treacherous terrain, consisting of small white stones that slid underfoot like a treadmill, had sorely tested the willpower of the office worker whose vacation had yet to begin.

With Anselmo's 4X4 off road vehicle, they had been able to cross the Piano della Gardosa, following the dirt road that went from the village of Foce up to a beech grove where the carriage road becomes a mule track. From there they'd gone by foot.

The woodcutter had insisted on equipment that was essential, but uncomfortable for someone who was not accustomed to the steep climb on a route that would take them over 3000 feet upwards. Hiking boots, a knapsack with a good supply of water, a windbreaker, and a hunting rifle with cartridges. At first Maurizio had refused to carry the weapon but Anselmo had made the ultimate threat of not accompanying him.

The gun weighed more than everything else.

The hollowed glacial basin that contained the lake was located at an altitude of 6364 feet, within a curved ridge made up of the highest peaks of the Sibillini: Monte Vettore, Cima del Redentore, Monte Argentella, and Palazzo Borghese. As the two men hiked up the U-shaped valley, Monte Sibilla towered behind their backs, scarred by the zig-zagging road which had been carved not long ago in the direction of the cave, the legendary dwelling of the queen of the oracles.

In truth the most popular itineraries for reaching the Lago di Pilato passed through Forca di Presta or Castelluccio di Norcia, both on the Umbrian versant. But for this very reason the two friends had chosen the more difficult trail. If Giulia turned out to be right, they would have the chance of surprising Morgana's kidnappers from the less predictable side.

Anselmo carried his favorite weapon, a Benelli Argo Comfortech hunting rifle, which used a 30-06 shell, the preferred cartridge for shooting wild boar, at one time American military issue equipment. He loved to hunt, and in addition to this powerful precision rifle, he owned five more guns of diverse calibers, all of them employed in the pursuit of his passion.

For Maurizio he had chosen a semiautomatic Beretta, model A 391 xtrema2, conceived and built for the use of supermagnum cartridges caliber 12 by 9mm. For this occasion it was accessorized with single ball munitions.

"Anselmo, I warn you, I'm not sure I'm capable of aiming this gun at someone, let alone firing it. And to tell the truth, I have no idea what to do in the face of danger. Plus, I don't even know what the hell we're doing here!"

The ex-alpinist could tell that fatigue was taking its toll on his companion, who stumbled along behind him, so he tried another distraction.

It really wasn't much further.

"You know something about shooting somebody? There's a big difference between hunting bullets and military bullets. What we have are for hunting, not war. Military bullets follow a particular criterion: they have to put the adversary out of action without totally wrecking his body. To this end the lead of the bullet is covered with a much harder jacket that won't change shape so much on impact, minimizing its destructive effects. The munitions used for hunting, however, follow the opposite criterion: the soft lead has to destroy, unload a maximum amount of energy so that the animal dies instantly, reducing its suffering to a minimum. So the bullet tends to deform itself a lot on impact with the body."

"And so? What are you saying?"

"That I have no intention of firing unless it's absolutely necessary. And it's only fair that you should know that."

Maurizio stopped for a few moments, staring at the ground. In his head the muffled sense of unreality was amplified by the rarified atmosphere of the high altitude.

He lifted his eyes to the sky. Just like him, it seemed undecided, grey clouds alternating with splashes of blue. When he looked back down, he realized that he could see the Lago di Pilato up ahead, just in front of them.

Ascoli Piceno
Mazzoni Hospital
Men's Orthopedic Ward
Thursday June 21, 20XX
11:51 AM

Three times in a row, Tony replayed the short video contained on the flashdrive.

Three times he shared with Giulia the surprising excerpt from TG3 Marche, dated November 2005, that Angelo Di Pietro had tracked down regarding Ecosystem.

The TV clip profiled the big firm, headquartered in Ascoli Piceno, at the peak of its economic success. The reporter lauded the company for the important occupational capacity put at the disposition of the zone, praised it for its many undertakings in the fields of ecology and the environment, held it up as an example of the industriousness of the entire region. Specifically, it was the president of the corporation, seen during a press conference called on the occasion of a capital increase, who personified the qualities of the Piceno firm.

Augusto Piloni de Castris.

Neither of them could figure out how to place this information in the context of the bloody events unfolding in these hours.

Why would such a highly successful businessman transform himself into a possessed follower of pagan rituals, crazed to the point of becoming a merciless killer?

Giulia and Tony couldn't avoid noting certain truly disturbing coincidences: the Count, head of a violent sect, who first used an excuse to get close to Morgana, inviting her to his party and then asking for her hospitality in Montegallo; Maurizio's house, also in Montegallo, object of a legal dispute with Ecosystem; the water, considered sacred by the killers, at the center of the shady illegal dealings between the mayor of Montegallo and one of the victims.

Common denominator, Montegallo; its territory, its springs, its myths, its politics, even its economy.

There seemed to be no apparent connection between the Count's business dealings and his role as a spiritual guide, a role that had made him the instigator of five murders. Or maybe there was a link between the crimes committed by the Brotherhood of the Oracles and the activities of Ecosystem?

Montemonaco
Lago di Pilato
Thursday June 21, 20XX
12:04 PM

What happened in the next half hour was beyond anything they could've foreseen.

At least for Maurizio Verdimani, employee in the RAI archive, lover of painting and music.

A calm man with a calm life. Up until a week ago.

Arriving at last in the proximity of the Lago di Pilato, they had stopped.

The pause, part of Anselmo's plan, allowed them to observe the predetermined goal from a safe distance.

The ex-soldier's caution proved to be more than advisable.

The lake shore swarmed with men and women dressed in white, just like Giulia and Tony had described, but without the Ku Klux Klan hoods.

Anselmo made a sign to Maurizio to get down.

They stretched out on the ground behind the rocks. With binoculars, the woodcutter set about examining the scene.

Giulia had guessed right.

A hundred people stood on the cobbled bank of the lake. On the spit of land that emerged every summer at the center of the mirror of water, dividing it almost completely into two basins, four men dragged a struggling woman closer to a white stone. On the other side of the stone, a bald fellow with some sort of two edged ax in his hand solemnly assisted in subduing the victim. Around his thin neck writhed a garland of snakes.

After staring at the scene for a few seconds, Anselmo passed the binoculars to Maurizio. Maurizio shivered. Signora Bucci was forced to kneel in front of the Count Piloni de Castris, to place her head on the stone with her arms behind her back. The four men held her firmly in this position.

The Count seemed to be intent on reciting some ritual formula, but the ax he held in his hand did not promise a good outcome.

Maurizio, already in shock, was surprised to find himself thinking about the final scene in "Salo, 120 Days of Sodom." The pitiless hierarchs who watched through binoculars as the young hostages were subjected to terrible violence . . .

Anselmo shook him.

"Get on your phone and call the Carabinieri."

"Of course, you're right."

The call went through. It took a while to make himself understood, but eventually he was able to extract the promise of a swift intervention.

But he wasn't satisfied. In fact, he was terrified. The tone of the voice on the other end left him feeling that he had gotten only token reassurance.

Another idea came to him. He called Giulia's number.

She answered on the first ring.

He summarized as best he could the state of affairs and asked her to telephone Marshal Moser right away.

Giulia didn't take it calmly. She started by screaming that

Moser would never get there in time. "Those idiots are all tied up setting a trap at the Santuario dell'Ambro. You two have to do something! Now!"

"But what are you saying? There's at least a hundred of them."

At that point Maurizio heard another incredible story.

The reporter told him about the video, that the Count was the president of Ecosystem and in all likelihood the sect's activities were connected to the firm's business. And she also told him — maybe exaggerating — that it was Piloni de Castris who wanted to take away his house.

As the coup de grace, she told him that she would hold him, Maurizio Verdimani, solely responsible for the death of Morgana Bucci.

Maurizio hung up.

He kept looking, without the binoculars, towards the Lago di Pilato.

Then he whispered a phrase that not even Anselmo could hear, "I always thought you were an asshole!"

Montemonaco
Lago di Pilato
Thursday June 21, 20XX
12:23 PM

"There's a thunderstorm coming," said the bearded man who was twisting Morgana's arms behind her back, forcing her to remain painfully crouched on her knees.

In front of her loomed the Count.

With a menacing air, he towered above her, raising to his shoulder the long-handled double ax.

Distant thunder confirmed the prediction. Gusts of cold wind slapped the victim's face, pressed forcibly against the surface of the big stone.

The expert on esoterics knew that the flat rock was a sacrificial alter, that the mysterious letters carved on its surface were ancient demonic invocations, but never, not even in her worst nightmares, could she have imagined that one day she would be forced to examine it this close up. And in a way that left no room for doubt.

The Count Augusto Piloni de Castris began to offer up incomprehensible words.

His followers responded with phrases just as enigmatic, an undecipherable litany that soon became a blood-chilling dirge. Mystical and absorbing for everybody present but unbearable for Morgana who, although she didn't know the meaning of the singsong, understood very clearly what it was leading up to: the moment of the summer solstice when the Count would cut off her head, extract her pineal gland, and eat it.

All at once, silence. Sudden, heavy, total.

Everyone was quiet.

A moment suspended in eternity took possession of that world set at the summit of the most tragic and secret superstitions; spirituality brought down by ridiculous human ambitions.

Interminable seconds with the wind providing an ominous background. Thunder, much louder than before, echoed down the valley.

The Great Master—alias the Count Augusto Piloni de Castris, alias president of Ecosystem—immersed his right hand in the lake, passed it over Morgana's forehead, grasped the handle of the double headed ax and lifted it over his head.

The image of the double blades silhouetted against the thunderclouds struck the eyes of the woman prostrate at his feet.

She thought it might be the last thing she ever saw in her life.

Nooo!

The survival instinct drove her to make one last attempt. She tried to escape from the grip of the bearded acolyte who was still behind her, holding her tight.

She tried with everything she had, with every single fiber of her body, with every single particle of her being. She tried beyond any hope, because it was the only thing left to do.

Try.

Right at the moment of maximum effort—sustained by the most disheartened desperation—a shot broke the silence that up until then had enveloped the entire valley.

Almost at the same moment the man behind the victim let out a cry, loosened his grip, and fell to the ground clutching his left knee with his bloodied hands.

Morgana dodged the ax blow.

The edge of the blade crashed on the stone in an explosion of sparks.

More shots. The Brotherhood turned towards the sound.

Someone was running at them firing a rifle into the air.

The Count, after the initial surprise, raised the ax again with the intention of completing the sacrifice.

Having avoided the first attempt, Morgana still found herself on the ground, surrounded by the waters of the lake, with her hands and feet tied. She couldn't do anything except glare helplessly at her executioner as he got in position to decapitate her.

He stretched his arm overhead, the ax pointing towards the clouds.

A lightning bolt shot forth, darting across the sky.

With inexorable precision, it struck the blade.

Augusto Piloni de Castris was transformed into a lightning rod, the electrical charge coursing through him before the astonished gaze of his disciples.

Immobilized for some fractions of a second, his body vibrated violently and a contorted expression transfigured his face. His eyes rolled, his mouth was distorted in an unnatural grimace and he dropped to the ground. The necklace of snakes coiled, motionless, on his chest.

The smell of burning meat.

"Nobody move!"

Two more shots.

Morgana recognized Maurizio. He came ever closer, ever more determined. The crowd, on the contrary, was dumbfounded, paralyzed by the unexpected sequence of events.

"Nobody make a move! I'm not alone!" yelled the improvised hero, not very convincingly.

A dozen of the Brotherhood showed signs of courage, moving to encircle the gunman. Another shot whistled through the air.

One of the dozen fell to the ground with a hole in his right thigh.

Another shot. Another man on the ground, this time wounded in the ankle.

Excellent deterrent.

Everyone put their hands up.

With ill-concealed nervousness Maurizio made his way through the middle of the assembly.

Using the tongue of land as a gang plank, he reached Morgana at the center of the lake. He freed her from the ties that held her wrists and ankles, and helped her to her feet. They walked north, retraced Maurizio's steps.

Two men started to follow them but were stopped by a bullet fired into the earth. This time the sniper had aimed a few steps in front of the pursuers.

For a few minutes Morgana and Maurizio marched at full speed, without turning, until they reached Anselmo. The woodcutter was stretched on the ground with a carbine armed with a telescopic sight, keeping the throng of confused pagans in his sights.

A knot of people had already formed around the body of the Grand Master. Others were organizing with the aim of following the fugitives.

All at once the entire valley seemed to be ringed by men dressed in grey.

The Forest Rangers.

PART FOUR

Friday June 22, 20XX

IL MESSAGGERO MARCHE
COUNT AUGUSTO PILONI DE CASTRIS
LEADER OF A BLOODY SECT!

Incredible developments in "The Crimes of the Sibillini" news story.

The noted businessman and aristocrat Augusto Piloni de Castris died yesterday morning. While on the point of sacrificing the latest victim in a series of murders, the Count was struck by a bolt of lightning that hit the blade of the ax he was holding. Allegedly he was about to decapitate the designated victim, Morgana Bucci. The Brotherhood of the Oracles—a frenzied cult that worships the waters and springs of the Sibillini Mountains—had gathered on the banks the Lago di Pilato to carry out an ancient pagan rite with the aim of gaining the power to foretell the future. The climax of the occult ceremony would have been the beheading of the "preselected" victim at the exact moment of the summer solstice and the ingestion of her pineal gland, also called the "third eye."

This blood curdling finale was prevented thanks to the intervention of the agents of the State Forest Service, who arrived at the location following an ongoing investigation developed in cooperation with the Carabinieri. Many of the details remain unclear, but the investigators have verified the direct involvement of the Brotherhood of the Oracles in the murders of this week, committed with the aim of blocking the concession of Montegallo's water resources, considered sacred by Count Piloni de Castris and his followers, to Silvio Forlan's firm Acque Sane.

President of Ecosystem during the day, Grand Master of the

Brotherhood of the Oracles after sunset, Count Piloni de Castris was the occult mind hidden behind these acts of unprecedented ferocity. This revelation has dismayed all those who had known and esteemed him as an entrepreneur and as a representative of the local aristocracy.

Giulia Cantarini

Montegallo
Village of Astorara
Friday June 22, 20XX
8:33 AM

"Noooo! Enough! I can't take it anymore."

Maurizio didn't even realize that he was talking to himself, with his head sandwiched between two pillows in an attempt to block the noise that came from outside. For the third time a truck's motor shook the glass in the windows.

The dirt road that these accursed monsters rumbled up and down, with ever greater frequency, passed right below his bedroom.

Maurizio tossed and turned between the sheets trying to fall back asleep. He had been flailing around since 3 AM, when his sleepless night had started with an earthquake tremor.

The last days had been a heavy load, exhausting and extraordinarily unpredictable.

The vacation had been ever less of a vacation.

Montegallo, the National Park of the Sibillini, his house, the surrounding fields and woods, everything seemed so different from how he remembered it.

But really, truck traffic... what the hell!

He got up, splashed water on his face, and opened the phonebook.

He found the number of the town hall.

"Hello! Good morning, this is Maurizio Verdimani."

"Who?"

"Verdimani, Maurizio Verdimani. Listen, I would like some

information about the trucks that have been driving through the village of Astorara every day. I live..."

"Yes, ahem, I'll transfer you to the technical office."

He waited for more than a minute. When he was about to hang up he heard the click of the receiver being lifted on the other end.

"Hello..."

"Who am I speaking to?"

"The surveyor Franchi. What can I do for you?"

"Good morning, my name is Maurizio Verdimani, I live in Astorara and I'm calling about the trucks that keep going past my house on the dirt road from Astorara up towards the Fonte Graniera."

"Towards the landslide. Fonte Graniera doesn't exist anymore."

The nit-picking correction got on his nerves. The civil attitude that he had maintained up until this moment was swept away by a burst of anger.

"That's not the point. I want to know for what fucking reason, for days, at all hours, especially at night, these monsters drive up a road that's really nothing more than a muletrack, making a hellacious racket... polluting like a smokestack an area that, as far as I know, is in the middle of a national park... what the hell are these trucks doing there?"

"Signor Verdimani, calm down."

"What do you mean, calm down? You try..."

"Listen, the heavy machinery belongs to the firm repairing the area devastated by the landslide. And given that, as you have rightly said, we are inside a park, the work of securing and repairing the location must be completed following precise criteria of environmental engineering."

"It better be! Otherwise what would they be building? A lovely shopping center all cement and glass?"

"Signor Verdimani, the firm that's performing the work is the best there is in the field of environmental engineering, in the maintenance of areas of great ecological interest. Ecosystem..."

"What? What did you say was the name of the firm?

"Ecosystem."

Ascoli Piceno
Mazzoni Hospital
Women's Ward
Friday June 22, 20XX
9:16 AM

The only other bed in the room was covered with the newspapers that had been brought at her request since early morning.

Relieved by the good news regarding Morgana's condition — the authorities had sent her to recover in a private clinic to protect her from overeager journalists — Giulia was dedicating herself to the difficult task of putting in order the numerous pieces of a confusing puzzle.

Special assistant: Tony Liberati.

Still in pain from the two broken ribs, he was seated at the table where the attendants normally set down the food trays. He kept watching the transmission of TG Regional that Maurizio's colleague, Angelo Di Pietro, had tracked down regarding Ecosystem. Once he had gotten over the surprising discovery that the Count was the president, he was drawn to something else.

"Hey! This will be the twentieth time you've looked at that piece. It's just an ordinary interview. That lunatic doesn't say anything unusual."

"It's not him, it's the other people there."

"The interview was part of a press conference called at the end of an assembly of shareholders in which a stock sale was decided. The people standing behind the Count could be other executives of the firm, or proprietary partners with important amounts of capital."

"I think I recognize the woman to the right of the Count, only I can't quite remember from where . . . bah, maybe it's just an impression."

Giulia stopped fussing with her friend's cellphone, on which she too had been watching the same film for the hundredth time — the half-naked confidences of Senator Emidio Cecchini to Tony Liberati, porn star version.

She got up from her bed and looked over his shoulder.

Without turning around Tony indicated the face he was referring to.

Giulia bent over, getting her eyes closer to the fixed image.

"You're right. And I can tell you who she is!"

"You know her?"

"Of course, I remember she was at another press conference,
the one held in Montegallo's town hall."

"The mayor's wife!" they said in unison,

Tony ran his hands through his hair. "Yes yes! I'm sure of it, I
remember seeing her at the Count's party at the Caffe Meletti too.
But what does it mean?"

Giulia withdrew her gaze from the screen and went to look
outside.

The fifth floor picture window framed on the skyline the rocky
body of Mt. Vettore: seen from afar it looked like a giant stretched
out in a sleep full of peaceful dreams.

Just an illusion.

The journalist knew well how illusory that serenity could be,
evoked by that skyline. She remained lost in thought for a few moments before answering.

"It's hard to say. The fact is that we have many strange elements at our disposal that don't fit together. I don't understand
what connection there could be between a noble millionaire obsessed with esotericism, ready to do anything to defend the object of
his cult—the springs of the Sibillini—and a corrupt mayor and a
corrupting businessman who were blocked from completing a shady
deal involving the same springs. Plus the Count is also the president of an important business enterprise that operates in the sector
of ecology and the environment, and this same business somehow
involves the wife of the corrupt mayor—specifically corrupted to
give away the indiscriminate exploitation of precisely those springs
that the Count wants to conserve free from commercial ties. I just
don't understand. Apparently Piloni de Castris had an absurd fixation on the Sibillini waters, seeing as how there's no link between
the Sibillini territory and Ecosystem and therefore with the may-
or's wife, who, on the contrary, should be on the same side as her
husband, and his objective was to entrust the exploitation of the

springs to Forlan...but the sect's crimes were always aimed at stopping him. Wait! There is a link, even if it's really weak. Ecosystem wants to acquire Maurizio's house, regardless of the cost, but why? I don't understand. I don't see the connections between the facts, even though they must be there. They can't just be coincidences. There are too many! I don't believe that..."

Tony listened in silence to Giulia's soliloquy, addressed to nobody in particular.

Or maybe not. She was addressing Mt. Vettore and its nightmares.

A nurse brought them back to their condition as in-patients.

"The head doctor is making his rounds. Signor Liberati, you must go back to your room, you must also..."

She didn't finish the sentence because her gaze fell on Tony's cell phone, still on the bed with the video function activated. The Senator being sodomized by Lady T, emphasizing his predicament with cries and grimaces of difficult interpretation.

"I'm going right away." He passed in front of the head nurse, who was hypnotized by the images that continued to run on the small screen.

Retrieving his cell phone, he turned to her with a smile and a comment. "Dear lady...you see how he suffers!"

Montegallo
Village of Astorara
Friday June 22, 20XX
9:28 AM

Maurizio decided to get some air.

Leaving his house, he found himself walking along the same road taken by the Ecosystem's black trucks, the road that went up towards the Fonte Graniera.

He remembered this route; when he was a kid he had gone this way with his father.

Papa Salvatore had suffered from high blood pressure, but found that drinking the water that gushed from the old fountain had a very beneficial effect. Probably the diuretic properties of this water facilitated the elimination of liquids, thus lowering the blood pressure, but his old dad wasn't interested in medical reasons: he knew that this spring was miraculous, and that was enough for him.

A profound sadness assailed Maurizio at the thought that following the big landslide of 2003 the fountain had disappeared and the precious spring was buried. Certainly the water hadn't vanished into nothingness, but who knew through what vein it now coursed in the heart of the mountain.

Another piece of his life — apparently solid and reassuring — shattered over time by Nature, always more honest than the illusions on which human ambitions are founded. In a flash his mind grasped the contrast between the ending of things, the inexorable and continuous change of existence, and the human incapacity to accept this ending, whatever it might be and in whatever form it might manifest itself.

Individuals forced by this incapacity to fight an exhausting battle, insane, already lost at the outset...

He smiled.

What strange ideas were passing through his head.

Maybe it was the fault of the pure air, a jolt of oxygen that he wasn't used to.

Step by step, he was getting closer to the huge landslide, an unhealed wound on the side of Mt. Vettore.

The rumble of a motor shattered the perfect state of grace into which he had been accidentally raised.

Another truck roared past. The backdraft buffeted him, but he hurried forward until he arrived at an immense patch of flat untilled land. He realized now that he was in the middle of the wound — inflicted not just by the landslide, but also by humans. Maybe it had been the removal of masses of detritus that had created this surreal landscape of earth, mud, and rocks. Huge blocks, probably too big to be removed, silently watched over the entire area, funeral monuments in memory of what had been.

No sign of the truck, not even a shadow.

Strange. The road ended at this large lot. Beyond that, nothing. Just the side of the mountain.

While he tried to come up with an explanation, he heard the usual noise rising from the valley. He hid himself.

The truck appeared. It slowed down, stopped for a few seconds—enough time for the mountain to open wide a huge mouth, engulf the truck, and then return to what it always had been.

Rock and nothing more.

But this wasn't just rock.

A door, camouflaged within the rocky rib, had momentarily moved to one side, probably running on a track.

Incredulous, Maurizio tried to make sense of it. Everything passed through his mind, but nothing plausible. He decided to take action.

Creeping cautiously, he hid behind another pile close to the mysterious entrance. For several seconds, fear had the upper hand. Then, when the door opened again to let the truck out, curiosity took over. The irresistible urge forced him to sneak inside. A foolhardy move on his part, but he thought of that only when he heard the metallic clang of the door closing behind him.

In front of him stretched a huge tunnel. Lights fixed in the vaulted cement ceiling allowed a certain visibility. It was cold, a damp cold.

Checking his cellphone, he found no signal. He started to walk.

Everybody knew that there were caves and cavities inside Vettore, caused by subterranean streams. But for sure, nobody imagined that there was this. All this.

Who knew how much work had been done here...

After hundreds of feet he approached the end of the tunnel. A more intense and diffuse light shone, beckoning him on.

He quickened his pace.

What he saw was truly chilling.

Ascoli Piceno
Mazzoni Hospital
Men's Orthopedic Ward
Friday June 22, 20XX
10:51 AM

The bribe had already been paid!

But of course...

Tony remembered perfectly what Senator Cecchini had said to him. That Forlan had called him on the phone to complain about the shameless behavior of Montegallo's mayor, who had expected the delivery of the wad of money at the restaurant that same evening.

The fact that Forlan was killed on his way back from the restaurant where he'd handed over the money meant one thing: from the mayor's point of view, the deal was wrapped up.

He had to talk to Giulia right away. Leaping out of bed, a stab of pain reminded him of his two broken ribs. He grabbed his phone and left the room.

The reporter was sitting in bed with her laptop.

After he shared his revelation, they watched the video again.

There was no mistake.

Trying to take stock of the situation, it seemed like the cards on the table had changed a little, but not enough to explain everything.

For the mayor the elimination of the businessman — an inconvenient accomplice for whom he had to fulfill well defined obligations — may have been an advantage. However, for Count de Castris, committing the crime was a useless risk.

Why the Ascolano aristocrat would have decided to run this risk remained a mystery.

Unless he was truly possessed by the irresistible desire to sacrifice a human life — or two — in one of the churches of the constellation of the Virgin.

Unless the true target was Simona Coda, or to be precise, her pineal gland.

In any case, the count's insanity was still the only motive. The role of Ecosystem, given that there was one, was still unknown. The question that had to be answered: why was Ecosystem against the exploitation of Montegallo's waters by Forlan's Acqua Sane?

They decided to notify the authorities.

Marshal Moser's phone was off.

So they called the provincial command post.

Giulia tried to get through to Major Baracca; she remembered him from the press conference at town hall. No luck. She left a message.

After a couple of minutes, Marshal Fianchini called them back: he was the one who had interrogated Tony following the accident with the SUV on the night of the first murder.

They summarized their suspicions as clearly as they could.

Fianchini seemed skeptical: he would let them know.

He hung up.

Tony's disappointment was visible.

Giulia was almost ready to drop it. Maybe she'd made a wild guess in the hope of finding an interesting development in what was basically a simple crime story, the result of a tragic mental disorder.

"I'm sorry I got you involved in this business," she turned to Tony, fixing her eyes on his. "I've put you in danger on account of my foolish ambition. I made you risk your life just to . . . to . . . chase a stupid scoop . . . and you were very brave."

Tony wasn't even listening. He was too carried away, floating in those eyes. A different expression, which he had never seen before.

She kept talking, interrupting herself from time to time. "And you're still here, searching for new leads. You're really . . ."

"Listen to me. It's not like that. We were right to go in there. Morgana was in serious danger and those were some crazy killers. And I didn't do it for you, that is . . . I did it also for you, but I did it because I felt and still feel that it was the right thing to do, and you know what I have to tell you? It's been years since I felt this good! Like I did something that was important, not just for me, and that's fantastic."

For some seconds they looked at each other in silence. Then Giulia kissed him. They kissed for a long time.

They were still kissing when a voice from the laptop stopped them.

"Mamma! Mamma! How are you?"

Montegallo
Fonte Graniera Zone
Friday June 22, 20XX
11:08 AM

Maurizio raised his hand to his mouth.

Amazement, horror, and disgust in a single gesture.

He found himself at the entrance of an enormous cavern, with another two parallel tunnels leading off on the right side.

The cavern was not empty.

Strewn everywhere were tall heaps of drums, kegs, casks, barrels and containers of every sort marked with the unmistakable symbols of dangerous toxic waste.

Yellow triangles with skulls; stylized fans that indicated radioactive waste; orange icons that described the various characteristics of the noxious chemical substances to which they referred. A nauseating stench dominated the motionless air. Many of the drums lay on the ground, some broken. Fluorescent liquids seeped over the earth, on the stones, and also into a pair of streams that flowed through the cave.

The three black vehicles parked on the left seemed empty. The surrounding space was completely lifeless. Nothing, not even an insect, moved within this vision worthy of a circle of hell.

The diseased silence encouraged Maurizio to take a few steps forward.

He felt his feet sink into the mud.

A green slush had soaked his shoes.

He stopped, took out his cell phone, and used it as camera. Otherwise, who would ever believe him? While taking the pictures he felt his heartbeat accelerate. A spasm of retching forced him to stop. He bent his legs and regurgitated gastric juices. That liquid seemed to him the healthiest substance present here.

"It really is disgusting, isn't it?"

He recognized the voice and turned around. "Marshal..."

Marshal Francesco Moser stood behind him with his hands in the pockets.

He wasn't wearing his uniform.

"The common saying is that mountain walks are good for your health, but that isn't always the case."

"Marshal! How lucky..."

"Stop! Don't move. Stay where you are."

Moser pulled out his pistol and pointed it at Maurizio.

"But what does this mean?"

"It means that you should never have come here. And further, that you never did."

The officer, at the threshold of the main tunnel, held his weapon level and ready to shoot.

Maurizio hadn't heard him arrive.

Maurizio wanted to leave, but he had been told not to move.

Maurizio looked down at his shoes — the Clarks were immersed in a glowing liquid of a nasty green color.

Maurizio realized he was afraid, and that scared him even more.

Maurizio talked just to be doing something. "So then you knew all about this..."

Maurizio was not doing a very good job of displaying his insightfulness. He could have done better.

Moser answered, "Dear Signor Verdimani, I'm only a pawn...a willing one, but still just a pawn. A part of the system. You are probably thinking: but how can a Carabiniere be an accomplice in something so disgusting? You're right, but it happened like this. They pay me well to keep an eye on this place and what can I say? I've got a family. It started by chance and at first it was just a couple of drums. That didn't seem very serious to me, sometimes the law is a matter of interpretation. Just a couple of drums, I thought, what harm are they doing? I've been polluted too — corrupted some would say — and then Ecosystem pays well... but I already told you that..."

"Marshal, people have been killed!"

"But I didn't know Ecosystem was in the middle of that. I

truly believed that the guilty party was some lunatic. In fact at the beginning I was completely convinced that by following the Virgo clues I would arrest the killer or killers. Basically that was true. I didn't know Piloni de Castris — who, indeed, has been shown to be out of his mind — and I certainly didn't know that he was the boss of the Ecosystem. I don't say that to justify myself, it's the truth. I found out the day after the murders of Silvio Forlan and Simona Coda, after I asked for Signora Cantarini's help. That morning when I came looking for her at your house, I was still in the dark about the connection between Ecosystem and the murders. I was brought up to date in the afternoon of that same day."

"And who told you?"

Moser cracked a smile. "The mayor."

"Why?"

"So that I wouldn't interfere with the Count's plans. That's why I directed everybody's attention to the Santuario dell'Ambro. Like I told you ... I'm only a pawn after all ..."

"I meant, why these deaths? Why didn't Ecosystem want Forlan to undertake the management of the springs? What did they matter to Ecosystem?"

"What, you still don't understand? Because of this area, because of Fonte Graniera! The Fonte Graniera spring is the most important of all those that would've been handed over by the town concession. Forlan would have certainly tried to excavate the original spring buried by the landslide ..."

Maurizio completed the idea. "But he would have then discovered a huge illegal dump of toxic waste. An environmental disaster of monstrous proportions."

"Congratulations, Verdimani, now you understand everything."

"To tell the truth, there are a lot of things I don't understand. What does the mayor have to do with Ecosystem? From what I know Assergi was in cahoots with Forlan in the water business ..."

"That's enough now."

"Why did you tell me all these details?"

"I don't know, maybe I needed to explain to someone ... or to myself ... the reason why I've become what I am: a servant of the law who has put the law into his own service. In any case, I told it to someone who won't ever be able to tell anybody."

Francesco Moser cocked the hammer of his 9mm Beretta.

Ascoli Piceno
Piazza del Popolo
Friday June 22, 20XX
11:17 AM

"Good morning, Mayor!"

"Good morning, buddy!"

Fabiano Assergi strolled serenely across the piazza, where he had always dreamed of making a star appearance. The office he held in Montegallo had finally given him sufficient fame in Ascoli to gratify his frustrated ego.

"Hey Mayor! Looking good, huh?"

"We're doing our best, thanks."

The latest news reports had made him known even among people unlikely to visit the mountain region.

"Mayor! How's it going in Montegallo?"

"Much better now, thanks. It's been tough, but we made it through."

The sense of inadequacy that he had always felt and had never confessed to anyone, not even to himself, was now stilled, as he found himself rewarded with social success, sudden wealth, and — why not? — a touch of fame.

Basically, for him, everything had turned out for the best. Life goes on.

"Good day, Mayor. Give my regards to the missis."

"Thanks, I'll do that."

Business went on. Even his wife seemed to be cheering up, in fact she was actually happy.

Of course. Ecosystem was a gold mine. If he'd known about it sooner, he could've avoided a lot of trouble.

He reached the short end of the Piazza del Popolo — bordered by the church of San Francesco—having crossed the square three times in a sort of personal promenade.

He had enjoyed the greetings and the compliments. He glowed under the curious glances of those who, lacking in confidence, limited themselves to watching him. He accepted as gifts the whispered comments of passersby incapable of discretion.

He was pleased by all of it.

He thought it might almost be enough.

He walked towards the right and then back towards the left.

He was skirting the church of San Francesco again, on the Via d'Ancaria, when he checked the time on his wristwatch.

He made a mental note to buy a more expensive one.

The hands pointed to 11:22.

Fabiano Assergi felt the earth tremble under his feet.

He heard cries of panic.

He saw people running.

He stood stock still, frozen by fear or maybe only by indecision. He didn't know where to go.

Stained glass fell from the gothic-style double arched windows.

He moved a little towards the center of the street.

The tremor seemed like it would never end.

He looked up.

He found himself below one of the two hexagonal bell towers. Below the north bell tower, the one with the unmistakable travertine phallus erected on a balustrade at the top of the tower.

The bell tower appeared to sway.

The prick seemed to tilt.

The mayor's survival instinct told him to run, but he didn't have time.

He remained paralyzed watching the mighty stone cock that fell towards him like a guided missile.

A fraction of a second in which to understand that he would die battered by the blow of a stone organ sculpted by the master stonemason Matteo Roberti in the fifteenth century.

The travertine projectile shattered his cranium.

In the following months, the fate of Mayor Fabiano Assergi was often described as the death of a real dickhead.

PART FOUR

Montegallo
Fonte Graniera Zone
Friday June 22, 20XX
11:21 AM

Maurizio knew he would never forget the vision of the small deadly black hole aimed at him, ready to cast him into the nothingness of an unexpected and unjust death.

A tear fell, fear materializing itself as liquid and salty.

Interminable seconds of silence forced him to think that this too was a useless reflection. Of course he would forget it. The dead have no memory.

The little black hole would be the last image of his life.

But it didn't turn out that way. Something happened that, as a matter of fact, he never would forget.

The earth began to tremble, the cavern to shake.

Fragments of rock fell from above.

Moser lost his balance, and Maurizio took advantage of this to escape.

Not in the direction from which he had come. The marshal blocked that way.

In the direction of the other tunnels.

The two pistol shots resounding with a terrifying echo made him understand that the slightest hesitation would be fatal.

He kept on running, desperate but uninjured. Moser had fired into the floor, his aim had been thrown off.

The earthquake kept on going too.

The continuous vibrations rose from the ground, travelled along the walls, pulsed through the vaulted ceiling, and penetrated even higher up, into the heart of a mountain violated by the greed and ignorance of unworthy humans.

Maurizio took refuge in the tunnel furthest to the left.

The cement which stabilized its walls seemed to be holding up.

Suddenly a dull roar rumbled through the grotto now flooded with sewage, with waste, with refuse of every type spilling from the barrels, the drums, all the containers toppled over from the heaps piled high with a consistent lack of skill.

The noise increased in intensity. It was coming from the mountain's flank, right in front of the main tunnel.

A gigantic mass of water exploded from the bowels of the earth.

The rock walls broke apart releasing a river of water and mud.

Maurizio took refuge in the side tunnel.

The tsunami hit Marshal Moser full force, hurling him violently down the corridor that led to the entrance.

The officer's scream was strangled in a terrible gurgle.

The earthquake had stopped, but the torrent kept flooding into the grotto. Maurizio preferred the risk of the unknown to a certain death.

He advanced into the tunnel. Total darkness. Using the display light from his cellphone he tried to figure out where it was leading him.

The roar of the water rushing into the grotto convinced him to pick up his pace. Unfortunately, given the darkness, running was out of the question.

Nevertheless, he had to hurry. The structure and slope of the cavern were such as to channel the mass of water towards the point where Moser had been, but it was obvious that quite soon the wave would flood back into his tunnel. The marginal advantage offered by its slightly elevated position was rapidly diminishing as the water level rose.

With his right hand he touched a metal object. A tube or something like that.

He stopped and pointed the display light at it.

A metal ladder! He started climbing. Maybe there was an emergency exit.

He clambered up, cautiously placing his weight on the rungs, testing their strength. They seemed solid enough. Not that he had any alternative.

Putting his phone in his pocket he proceeded in the dark.

The ladder entered an artificial shaft, narrow and even darker than the rest, if it's possible to give a gradation to total black.

He went on.

His head bumped something.

He touched the surface above him. Metal.

A few seconds of light from his cellphone revealed the truth.

It was a metal door.

A handle on the right filled him full of hope.

The strength of both arms was needed, but finally a click in the darkness made his heart leap.

He pushed with all the force he could muster, and the cover moved.

He re-emerged from the bowels of the earth. The sun blinded him for some instants, convincing him that he was saved.

Heaven knows! Truly born again!

- -

Saturday June 23, 20XX

IL MESSAGGERO MARCHE

EARTHQUAKE IN PICENO!
THREE DEAD AND DOZENS INJURED

The strong earthquake tremor which occurred yesterday at 11:22 AM, with its epicenter in the province of Ascoli Piceno, has claimed the lives of three victims. The dead have been identified as Fabiano Assergi, mayor of Montegallo; Francesco Moser, marshal of the Carabineiri; and Cesare Bonnani, a lawyer in Ascoli Piceno.

Mayor Assergi and the lawyer Bonanni lost their lives in Ascoli. The mayor was struck by debris falling from one of the bell towers of the church of San Francisco. The lawyer plunged from the terrace of his penthouse, his tumble apparently caused by a loss of balance due not just to the tremor, but also to a sudden violent blast of wind. Marshal Moser died in the territory of Montegallo, where he commanded the local Carabinieri station.

The involvement of the little mountain township, already the setting of recent acts of violence, is a disturbing coincidence.

Monday June 25, 20XX

CORRIERE ADRIATICO

MOUNTAIN POISONED
ENVIRONMENTAL DISASTER IN THE
NATIONAL PARK OF THE SIBILLINI

Friday's earthquake, which shook the province of Ascoli Piceno, has brought to light an illegal dump of dangerous toxic waste at the Fonte Graniera site in the mountain township of Montegallo, located in the heart of the National Park of the Sibillini.

Investigators have discovered an environmental disaster of unimaginable dimensions. A hiker, climbing a trail on the slopes of Mt. Vettore when the tremor occurred, alerted the authorities.

Still to be determined are those responsible for the criminal act. The noted environmental remediation firm Ecosystem has been implicated.

Ecosystem was recently in the headlines of the crime news because its President, Augusto Piloni de Castris, was found dead after taking part in a bloody ritual. The firm is being investigated regarding its responsibility for the restoration work of the area where the illegal dump was discovered.

Thursday July 5, 20XX

RESTO DEL CARLINO

ECOSYSTEM INVOLVED IN MASSIVE TRAFFIC OF TOXIC WASTE

SHOCKING DECLARATION FROM THE PROSECUTOR'S OFFICE OF ASCOLI

"THE MAIN PERPETRATORS ARE DEAD!"

In a press conference, the District Attorney of the Province of Ascoli Piceno, Ernesto Landini, announced, "From a first examination of the investigative report concerning the illegal dump in Montegallo, a complex situation has emerged which sees the interlacing of criminal ties on many levels. At the base of the criminal events lies a diabolical relationship of complicity between the economic lobby, conniving institutions, and corrupt representatives of the forces of order."

Still more shocking was the declaration by Dr. Landini that "The main perpetrators guilty in the Ecosystem affair have all died in recent days. Count Augusto Piloni de Castris, the mayor Fabiano Assergi, Marshal Francesco Moser, and the entrepreneur Silvio Forlan (this last a victim of the murderous fury of de Castris) have died at different times and in different ways, but all in the context of a bloody escalation unleashed by the mad quest for profits traceable to the highest echelons of Ecosystem."

Saturday July 7, 20XX

CORRIERE ADRIATICO

DIVINE PUNISHMENT!
LAWYER BONANNI ALSO
WORKED FOR ECOSYSTEM

Another disturbing development in the investigation of the eco-mafia in Le Marche. In addition to Mayor Assergi and Marshal Moser, the lawyer Cesare Bonanni, the third victim of the earthquake that shook the province of Ascoli Piceno at the end of the last month, is also implicated in the criminal activities of the economic colossus Ecosystem. Apparently Dr. Bonnani was an important legal consultant in the business headed by Count de Castris. The investigators have discovered this relationship only now because the lawyer was not directly tied to Ecosystem. He was not an employee but worked as an outside consultant on specific judicial controversies. The most recent of these involved the very area of Montegallo in which the Fonte Graniera dump was found. In violation of the legal code of ethics, the lawyer Bonanni had accepted the case of a client involved in a dispute with the same Ecosystem. Further investigations are underway regarding the wives of Bonanni and Assergi, both members of Ecosystem's board of Directors.

In the public mind the earthquake has punished the guilty.

Tuesday July 10, 20XX

IL MESSAGGERO MARCHE

A BOOK TELLS THE STORY
"BLOOD OF THE SIBILLINI"
OUR CORRESPONDENT GIULIA CANTARINI ANNOUNCES AN EXCLUSIVE SCOOP

In a surprise conference held in the bar of the hospital from which she had just been discharged, the journalist Giulia Cantarini announced the upcoming release of a book in which she tells the behind the scenes story of the Ecosystem scandal.

Our correspondent commented favorably on the workings of the investigators, but also left those present holding their breath when she claimed that "many details have not yet come out" and that "the mysteries that today are still unresolved will be revealed in my book entitled, 'The Blood of the Sibillini' available in all bookstores, coming this October...hopefully..." she concluded.

EPILOGUE

Ascoli Piceno
Villa San Bernardino Nursing Home
Monday August 20, 20XX
4:09 PM

Her cellphone rang as Giulia Cantarini passed through the gates of the institute managed by the Suore Ospedaliere, specializing in the care of patients affected by psychological disorders.

"Sara, what's up?

"Mamma, I can't find..."

"Listen Sara, this isn't a good time. I have an appointment and I'm late..."

"But mamma, I can't..."

"Hand me over to your grandmother."

"Giulia, I haven't been able to..."

"Whatever it is, I can't do anything about it. It's been an awful day. I just left a frustrating interview with the lawyer Bonanni's widow and now I'm going to see Giuseppe Grossi's sister. I've got an appointment at 3:30 with the director of Villa San Bernardino, but I'm just arriving now...so...I'll talk to you later."

She hung up.

Rushing, breathless, she arrived inside the building. Luckily Sister Giustina, the head of the institute, was in her office. Five minutes in the waiting room gave Giulia time to catch her breath.

The director proved to be cordial and helpful. She had organized a supervised visit with Andreina Grossi in the presence of herself and the psychologist Dr. Porzio. Giulia would be allowed to meet the sister of Giuseppe Grossi, who had killed himself after committing the first three in the bloody series of crimes.

But Sister Giustina had been clear. "The girl hasn't spoken since 1992, the year of the trauma. At that time they spoke of molestation; her preschool teacher was accused but later acquitted. Even today nobody knows who is responsible for poor Andreina's condition. She was five then, she's nineteen now, and in these fourteen years she hasn't uttered a word to anybody."

The reporter knew this story very well; it was the reason for her visit. Piloni di Castris had chosen Andreina's brother precisely for his smoldering hatred of the teacher Michela Angeletti. Given her relationship with Assergi she was considered the ideal sacrificial victim, her murder spotlighting an apparent hostility against the mayor and the concession of the water rights to Forlan. Perhaps Assergi's wife had also had a hand in it; after all, from her point of view, it could be considered a crime of honor.

For Giuseppe Grossi, perfect puppet in the hands of Ecosystem, it had been a simple and primordial vendetta.

Giulia reviewed these considerations for the hundredth time, in silence, refraining from commenting on the director's dry statement. Sister Giustina indicated that she should follow her, first into the elevator, then down a corridor that would bring them into Andreina's presence.

They entered a room on the fifth floor. Andreina Grossi was already waiting, in the company of Dr. Mariella Porzio.

She was sitting in a chair with her gaze fixed in space.

Giulia took another chair and placed it in front of the girl.

Trying to take a position that wasn't too aggressive, she set her purse on her knees and bent forward to create a confidential atmosphere.

"Hello, Andreina, how are you?" she asked softly.

But, nothing. Nothing happened.

Andreina continued to gaze at an indefinite point beyond the window.

Giulia leaned in, seeking make more direct contact.

She tried to take the girl's hand.

Her purse fell to the floor.

The thud woke Andreina from her torpor.

Out of the purse cascaded objects, papers, photographs.

Andreina started to tremble. She burst out crying without taking her eyes from the ground.

She spoke.

"It's him...It's him...It's him...It's him...It's him...It's him...It's him..."

The three women listened in silent amazement to the mantra chanted between tears and sobs, accompanied by a swaying movement of the young woman's torso which hit harder and harder against the back of her chair.

The photographs strewn on the floor showed various images: Forte Malatesta, the church of Santa Maria in Casalicchio, the frescoes in Santa Maria in Pantano, but only one face.

A closeup of the lawyer Bonanni.

In the hours that followed, Giulia Cantarini assisted in what Dr. Porzio called, to Sister Giustina's joy, a true miracle.

First in half sentences, then with greater eloquence, Andreina Grossi recounted that the person who had molested her was Bonanni.

It was during the chestnut harvest. She had been left alone, her mother had to go away for a half hour. She was supposed to wait for her there and gather chestnuts...at least that's what she remembered her mother telling her. That man said he was looking for mushrooms. He stayed there longer than a half hour.

That evening she felt bad. They took her to the hospital.

She didn't want to make any trouble so she didn't say anything, but in the hospital she wanted to draw something and a lady doctor asked her a lot of questions after she saw the drawings. Andreina was afraid of making her mother even angrier...Mamma had told her to gather chestnuts...and when she got back she was really mad because Andreina didn't have any chestnuts...so she didn't talk anymore.

The psychologist let her speak, intervening only when the pauses were too long. The reporter took notes. The director listened closely.

From the dates in her possession, Giulia knew that at the time of these events the lawyer Bonanni had immediately offered to take the child's case free of charge.

Up 'til now Giulia had thought that the lawyer was eager for the boost to his reputation that this highly charged case might provide. But suddenly the real motive became clear: Bonanni needed to be in control. He had been able to take full advantage of the muteness that poor Andreina had inflicted on herself.

Giulia left the Villa San Bernardino with an overwhelming desire to hug Sara.

Extract from the last page of the book

THE BLOOD OF THE SIBILLINI

I haven't seen Maurizio or Tony since.

Maurizio went back to Rome, to his work as an archivist, and he also returned to his real passion, painting. He sent me one; he had changed his style and subjects.

Now he is inspired by the Flemish master, Hieronymus Bosch.

The title of the painting is "The Seven Deadly Vices."

I haven't had any contact with Tony. From what Maurizio told me the last time he called, the actor hasn't changed his style. The latest news came from Brazil. Apparently he went there to participate in a reality show about immigrants…

Well!

Morgana is in great shape. By now she is considered an expert on the highest level in the field of esotericism and the paranormal. She's invited to conferences, holds seminars, but looks down on television. Bravo! Raise the price. She has already notified me that next year, at the summer solstice, she's going to the Lago di Pilato for a ritual thanksgiving to Mother Earth.

Senator Cecchini was investigated but he was cleared thanks to his parliamentary immunity. Now he's in a bit of trouble because he was caught with two hookers of indeterminate gender and sexual orientation, high on cocaine, yelling a declaration of war against Greece from a balcony.

That's everything.

A story made of crimes, corruption, madness, and ambition. But also a tale of how humans are the only animals capable of polluting themselves, their souls, the world around them, and the people they love.

It's second nature.

Our own nature.

THE END